THE YEAR OF
THE RANSOM

Books in the Millennium Series

POUL ANDERSON
THE YEAR OF THE RANSOM

ILLUSTRATED BY
PAUL RIVOCHE

MILLENNIUM

A BYRON PREISS BOOK

WALKER AND COMPANY
NEW YORK

THE YEAR OF THE RANSOM
Millennium™ Books

Cover painting by Paul Rivoche.
Book design by Alex Jay/Studio J.
Book edited by David M. Harris.

Special thanks to Ted Chichak and Amy Shields.

Library of Congress Cataloging-in-Publication Data

Anderson, Poul, 1926–
    The year of the ransom / Poul Anderson ; illustrated by Paul
Rivoche.
        p.   cm.—(A Millennium book)
    "A Bryon Preiss book."
    ISBN 0-8027-6800-8. ISBN 0-8027-6801-6 (pbk.)
    I. Title. II. Series.
PS3551.N378Y4   1988   87-29054
813.54—dc19   CIP

Printed in the United States of America.

10 9 8 7 6 5 4 3 2 1

THE YEAR OF
THE RANSOM

10 SEPTEMBER 1987

"Excellent loneliness." Yes, Kipling could say it. I remember how those lines of his rolled up and down my spine when first I heard them, Uncle Steve reading aloud to me. Though that must have been a dozen years ago, they still do. The poem's about the sea and the mountains, of course; but so are the Galápagos, the Enchanted Islands.

Today I need just a little of their loneliness. The tourists were mostly bright, decent people. Still, a season of herding them along the trails, answering the same questions over and over, does begin to wear on a person. Now they've become fewer, my summer job has ended, soon I'll be home Stateside, commencing grad school. Here is my last chance.

"Wanda, dear!" The word Roberto used is *querida*, which could mean quite a lot. Not necessarily. I wonder about it for a flicker or two while he says, "Please, at least let me come along."

Headshake. "I'm sorry, my friend." No, not exactly; *amigo* doesn't translate one-on-one into English, either. "I'm not sulking or anything. Far from it. All I want is a few hours by myself. Haven't you ever?"

I'm being honest. My fellow guides are fine. I wish the friendships I've made among them will keep. Surely they will if we can get back together. But that's uncertain. I may or may not be able to return next year. Eventually I may or may not make my dream of joining the research staff at Darwin Station. It can't take many scientists; or another dream could come along meanwhile and take me. This trip, on which half a dozen of us are knocking around the archipelago with a boat and a camping permit, may well be the end of what we've called *el compañerismo*, the Fellowship. Oh, I suppose a Christmas card or two.

"You need protection." Roberto has put on his dramatic style. "That strange man we heard of, asking around Puerto Ayora about the blonde young North American woman."

Let Roberto escort me? Temptation. He's handsome, lively, and a gentleman. We haven't exactly carried on a romance these past months, but we've gotten pretty close. While he's never told me in words, I know how much he's hoped we'd get closer yet. It hasn't been easy resisting.

Must be done, for his sake more than mine. Not because of his nationality. I think Ecuador is the Latin American country where most yanquis feel most at home. By our standards, things work right there. Quito is charming, and even Guayaquil— ugly, smog-choked, exploding with energy—reminds me of Los Angeles. However, Ecuador is not the U.S.A., and from its standpoint I've got a lot wrong with me, starting with the fact that I'm not sure when I'll be ready to settle down, if ever.

Therefore, laughing, "Oh, yes, Sr. Fuentes in the post office told me. Poor dear, how worried he was. The stranger's funny clothes and accent and everything. Hasn't he learned what can crawl off the cruise ships? And how many blondes do the Islands see, these days? Five hundred a year?"

"How would Wanda's secret admirer follow her, anyway?" Jennifer adds. "Swim?"

We happen to know that none of the ships has touched at Bartolomé since we left Santa Cruz; no yachts are nearby; and everybody would have recognized a local fisherman.

5

Roberto goes red under the tan we share. With pity, I pat his hand while telling the group, "Go ahead, folks, snorkel or whatever else you feel like. I'll be back in time for my share of supper chores."

Quickly, then, striding from the bight. I really do need some solitude in this weird, harsh, beautiful nature.

I could merge myself in it skindiving. The water's glass-clear, silky around me; now and then I see a penguin, not so much swimming as flying through it; fish dance like fireworks, seaweeds do a stately hula; I can get friendly with the sea lions. But other swimmers, never mind how dear they are, *will* talk. What I want is to commune with the land. In company I couldn't admit that. It'd sound too pompous, as though I were from Greenpeace or the People's Republic of Berkeley.

Now I've laid white-shell sand and mangroves behind me, I seem to have utter desolation underfoot. Bartolomé is volcanic, like its sisters, but bears hardly any soil. It's already hot beneath the morning sun; and never a cloud to soften the glare. Here and there sprawl gaunt shrubs or tussocks of grass, but they become few as I walk toward Pinnacle Rock. My Adidases whisper on dark lava, in simmering silence.

However . . . among boulders and tide pools, Sally Lightfoot crabs scuttle, brilliant orange-and-blue. Bound inland, I spy a lizard of a kind unique to this place. I'm within a yard of a blue-footed booby; she could flap off, but simply watches me, the naive creature. A finch flitting across my vision; it was the Galápagos finches that helped Darwin understand how life works through time. An albatross wheeling white. Higher cruises a frigate bird. Unship the binoculars hung at my neck and catch the arrogance of his wings in the spilling sunlight, the split tail like a buccaneer's twin swords.

Here are none of the paths I've generally required my tourists to stay on. Ecuadorian government strict about that. Given its all too limited resources, it's doing a great job trying to protect and restore the environment. Care where I put my feet, as becomes a biologist.

I'll circle around to the eastern end of the islet and there take the trail and stairs leading to the central peak. The view from the peak across to Santiago Island and widely over the ocean, is stunning; today I'll have it to myself. Probably that's where I'll eat the lunch I've packed along. May later go down to the cove, peel off shirt and jeans, enjoy a private dip before turning westward.

Careful about that, kid! You're a bare twenty klicks below the Equator. This sun wants respect. Tilt my hat brim against it and stop for a drink from my canteen.

Catch a breath, take a look around. I've gained some altitude, which I must give back before reaching the trailhead. Beach and camp are out of sight. Instead, I see a sweep and tumble of stone down to Sullivan Bay, fiery-blue water, Point Martínez lifting grayish on the big island. Is that a hawk there? Reach for the binoculars.

A flash in the sky. Light off metal. An airplane? No, can't be. It's gone.

Puzzled, I lower the glasses. I've heard enough about flying saucers, or UFOs, to give them the more respectable name. Never taken them seriously. Dad gave his children a healthy inoculation of skepticism. Well, he's an electronics engineer. Uncle Steve, the archaeologist, has knocked around a lot more in the world, and claims it's full of things we don't understand. I suppose I'll simply never know what it was I glimpsed. Let's push on.

Out of nowhere, a moment's gust. The air thuds softly. A shadow falls over me. I turn my face upward.

Can't be!

An outsize motorcycle, except every last detail is different, and it has no wheels, and it hangs there, ten feet up, unsupported, silent. A man in the front saddle grips what might be handlebars. I see him with knife sharpness. Each second takes forever. Terror has me, like nothing since I was seventeen, driving along the clifftops near Big Sur in a rainstorm, and the car went into a skid.

I pulled out of that one. This doesn't stop.

He's about five feet nine, rawboned but broad-shouldered, brown-skinned, pockmarked, hook-nosed, black hair falling past his ears, black beard and mustache trimmed to points, though getting shaggy. His outfit is what's absolutely wrong, on top of such a machine. Floppy boots, saggy brown hose poking out of short puffed breeches, long-sleeved loose shirt that might be saffron below its grime—steel breastplate, helmet, red cloak, sword scabbarded at left hip.

As if across a hundred miles: "Are you the lady Wanda Tamberly?"

Somehow that snaps me back from the edge of screaming. Whatever is going on, I can meet it. Hysteria never has been compulsory. Nightmare, fever dream? I don't believe so. The sun is too warm on my back and off the rocks, the sea too steadily bright, and I could count every spine on yonder cactus. Prank, stunt, psychological experiment? Less possible than the thing itself . . . His Spanish is the Castilian sort, but I never met that accent till now.

"Who are you?" I force out of my throat. "What are you after?"

His lips draw tight. Bad teeth. His tone is half

fierce, half desperate. "Quickly! I must find Wanda Tamberly. Her uncle Estebán is in terrible danger."

"I am she, " blurts my mouth.

He barks a laugh. His vehicle swoops down at me. Run!

He draws alongside, leans over, throws his right arm around my waist. Those muscles are titanium steel. Hauls me off my feet. That course I took in self-defense. My spread fingers jab for his eyes. He's too fast. Knocks my hand aside. Does something to a control board. Suddenly we're elsewhere.

3 JUNE 1533

(JULIAN CALENDAR)

This day the Peruvians brought to Caxamalca another load of the treasure that was to buy their king free. Luis Ildefonso Castelar y Moreno saw them from afar. He had been out exercising the horsemen under his command. They were now bound back, for the sun was low above western heights. Against shadows grown long throughout the valley, the river gleamed, and vapors turned golden as they rose from the hot springs of the royal baths. Llamas and human porters plodded in a line down the road from the south, wearied by burdens and many leagues. Natives stopped their labor in the fields to stare, then got hastily on with it. Obedience was ingrained, no matter who their overlord might be.

"Take charge," Castelar ordered his lieutenant, and put spurs to stallion. He drew rein just outside the small city and waited for the caravan.

A movement on the left caught his glance. Another man emerged afoot from between two white-plastered, thatch-roofed clay buildings. The man was tall; were both standing, he would top the rider by three inches or more. The hair around his tonsure was the same dusty brown as his Franciscan robe, but age had scarcely marked the sharp, light-complexioned visage—nor had the pox—and not a tooth was missing. Even after weeks and adventures, Castelar knew Fray Esteban Tanaquil. The recognition was mutual.

"Greetings, reverend sir," he said.

"God be with you," answered the friar. He stopped by the stirrup. The treasure train reached them and went on. Shouts of jubilation sounded from within the city.

"Ah," Castelar rejoiced, "a splendid sight, no?"

When he got no reply, he looked down. Pain touched the other face. "Is something wrong?" Castelar asked.

Tanaquil sighed. "I cannot help myself. I see how worn and footsore those men are. I think what a heritage of ages they carry, and how it has been wrung from them."

Castelar stiffened. "Would you speak against our captain?"

This was an odd fellow at best, he thought: beginning with his order, when the religious with the expedition were nearly all Dominicans. It was something of a puzzle how Tanaquil had come along in the first place, and eventually won the confidence of Francisco Pizarro. Well, that last must be due to his learning and gentle manners, both rare in this company.

"No, no, of course not," the friar said. "And yet—" His voice trailed off.

Castelar squirmed a bit. He believed he knew what went on beneath the shaven pate. He himself had wondered about the righteousness of what they did last year. The Inca Atahuallpa received the Spaniards peacefully; he let them quarter themselves in

Caxamalca; he entered the city by invitation, to continue negotiations; and his litter carried him into an ambush, where his attendants were gunned down and cut down by the hundreds while he was made prisoner. Now, at his bidding, his subjects stripped the country of wealth to fill a room with gold and another room twice with silver, the price of his liberty.

17

"God's will, " Castelar snapped. "We bring the Faith to these heathen. The king's well treated, isn't he? He even has his wives and servants to attend him. As for the ransom, Christ—" He cleared his throat. "Sant'Iago, like every good leader, rewards his troops well."

The friar cast a wry smile upward. It seemed to retort that preaching was not the proper business of a soldier. Outwardly, he shrugged and said, "Tonight I will see how well."

"Ah, yes." Castelar felt relief at sheering away from a dispute. No matter that he too once studied for holy orders, was expelled because of trouble with a girl, enlisted in the war against the French, at last followed Pizarro to the New World in hopes of whatever fortune the younger son of an impoverished Estremaduran hidalgo might find—he remained respectful of the cloth. "I hear you look every load over before it goes into the hoard."

"Someone should, someone who has an eye for the art rather than the mere metal. I persuaded our captain and his chaplain. Scholars at the Emperor's court and in the Church will be pleased that a fragment of knowledge was saved."

"Hm." Castelar tugged his beard. "But why do you do it at night?"

"You have heard that too?"

"I've been back for days. My ears are full of gossip."

"I daresay you give much more than you get. I'd like to talk with you at length myself. That was a herculean journey your party made."

Through Castelar passed a jumbled pageant of the months gone by, when Hernando Pizarro, the captain's brother, led a band west over the cordillera—stupendous mountains, dizzyingly deep ravines, brawling rivers—to Pachacamac and its dark oracular temple on the coast. "We had little gain," he said. "Our best booty was the Indio general Challcuchima. Get the lot of them together, under control . . . but you were going to tell me why you study the treasure only after sunset."

"To avoid exciting cupidity and discord worse than already afflict us. Men grow ever more impatient for division of the spoils. Besides, at night the forces of Satan are at their strongest. I pray over things that were consecrated to false gods."

The last porter trudged past and disappeared among walls.

"I'd like to see," Castelar said. Impulse flared. "Why not? I'll join you."

Tanaquil was startled. "What?"

"I won't disturb you. I'll simply watch."

Reluctance was unmistakable. "You must obtain permission first."

"Why? I have the rank. None would deny me. What have you against it? I should think you would welcome some company."

"You'll find it tedious. Others did. That is the reason they leave me alone at my task."

"I'm used to standing guard," Castelar laughed.

Tanaquil surrendered. "Very well, Don Luis, if you insist. Meet me at the Serpent House, as they're calling it, after compline."

—Stars glittered keen and countless over the uplands. Half or more of them were unknown to European skies. Castelar shivered and wrapped his cloak tighter around himself. His breath smoked; his boots rang on hard-packed streets. Caxamalca enclosed him, ghostly in the gloom. He felt glad of corselet, helmet, and sword, needless though they might seem here. Tavantinsuyu, the Indios called this land, the Four Quarters of the World; and somehow that felt more right than Perú, a name whose meaning nobody was sure of, for a realm whose reach dwarfed the Holy Roman Empire. Was it subdued yet, or could it ever entirely be, its peoples and their gods?

The thought was unworthy of a Christian. He hastened on.

The watchmen at the treasury were a reassuring

sight. Lantern glow sheened off armor, pikes, muskets. These were of the iron ruffians who had sailed from Panamá, marched through jungle and swamp and desert, shattered every foe, raised their strongholds, come in a handful, over a range that stormed heaven, to seize the very king of the pagans and lay his country under tribute. No man or demon would get past them without leave, nor stop them when again they fared onward.

They knew Castelar and saluted him. Fray Tanaquil was waiting, a lantern in his own hand. He led the cavalryman beneath a lintel sculpted in the form of a snake, though not such a snake as had ever haunted white men's nightmares, and into the building.

It was large, multiply chambered, of stone blocks cut and fitted together with exquisite care. The roof was timber, for this had been a palace. The Spaniards had supplied exterior entrances with stout doors, where the Indios had used curtains of reeds or cloth. Tanaquil shut the one through which he came.

Shadows filled corners and bobbed misshapen over wall paintings, which priests had piously defaced. Today's consignment lay in an anteroom. Castelar saw gleams beyond. He wondered half dizzily how many hundredweights of precious metal were heaped there.

He must content himself for the present with gloating over what he had seen arrive. Pizarro's officers had hastily unwrapped the bundles, to as-

sure themselves about the contents, and left everything where they tossed it. Tomorrow they would
weigh the mass and put it with the rest. Cords and
wrappings rustled under Castelar's boots, Tanaquil's sandals.

The friar set his lantern on the clay floor and
hunkered down. He picked up a golden cup,
brought it near the dim light, shook his head and
muttered. The thing was dented, the figures cast in
it crumpled. "The receivers dropped this, or kicked
it aside." Did anger tremble in his tone? "They've
no more care for workmanship than animals."

Castelar took the object from him and hefted it.
Easily a quarter pound, he reckoned. "Why should
they?" he asked. "It'll soon go to the smelter."

Bitterness: "True." After a moment: "They will
send a few pieces intact to the Emperor, for the sake
of whatever interest he may have. I've been picking
out the best, hoping Pizarro will listen to me and
choose them. But mostly he won't."

"What's the difference? Everything is just as
unsightly."

Gray eyes turned aloft to reproach the warrior.
"I thought you might be a little wiser, a little able to
understand that men have many ways of . . . prais-
ing God through the beauty they create. You have
an education, no?"

"Latin. Reading, writing, ciphering. A bit of
history and astronomy. It's largely dropped out of
me, I fear."

"And you've traveled."

"I fought in France and Italy. Gained a smattering of those languages."

"I have the impression you've acquired Quechua too."

"A minim. Can't let the natives play stupid, you know, or conspire in earshot." Castelar felt himself under inquisition, mild but probing, and changed 2 2 the subject. "You told me you record what you see. Where are your quill and paper?"

"I have an excellent memory. As you observed, there is not much point in itemizing things that are to become ingots. But to make sure no curse, no witchcraft lingers—"

Tanaquil had been sorting and arranging articles as he talked—ornaments, plates, vessels, figurines, grotesque in Castelar's sight. When they were marshalled before him, he reached inside a pouch hung at his waist and drew forth a curiosum of his own. Castelar stooped and squinted for a better look. "What's that?" he asked.

"A reliquary. It holds a fingerbone of St. Ippolito."

Castelar signed himself. Nonetheless he peered closer. "I've never seen its like." It was a hand's breadth in size, smoothly rounded, black save for a cross of nacreous material inset on top and, in front, two crystals more suggestive of lenses than of windows.

"A rare piece," the friar explained. "Left behind when the Moors departed Granada, later sanctified by these contents and the blessing of the Church. The bishop who entrusted it to me declared it has special efficacy against infidel magic. Captain Pizarro and Fray Valverde agreed it could be wise, and would certainly be harmless, if I subject each piece of Inca treasure to its influence.''

He assumed a more comfortable position on the floor, selected a small gold image of a beast, revolved it in his left hand before the crystals of the reliquary, which he held in his right. His lips moved silently. When he had finished, he put the object down and went on to another.

Castelar shifted from foot to foot.

After a while Tanaquil chuckled and said, "I warned you this would prove tedious. I'll be at it for hours. You may as well go to bed, Don Luis."

Castelar yawned. "I think you are right. Thank you for your courtesies."

A whoosh and thud brought him whirling around. For an instant he poised locked in unbelief.

Over by the wall, a thing had appeared. A thing—massive, dully slick, perhaps of steel, with a pair of handles and two stirrupless saddles. He saw it clear, for light radiated from a baton the rearmost rider held. Both men wore form-fitting black. It made their hands and faces stand forth bone-white, unweathered, unnatural.

The friar sprang up. He yelled. The words were not Spanish.

In that eyeblink of time, Castelar saw amazement on the aliens. Be they wizards or devils straight from Hell, they were not all-powerful, not before God and His saints. Castelar's sword whipped into his grasp. He plunged forward. "Sant'Iago and at them!" he roared, the ancient battle cry of his people as they drove the Moors from Spain back to Africa. Make such a racket that the guards outside would hear and—

24

The rider in front lifted a tube. It blinked. Castelar spun down into nothingness.

15 APRIL 1610

Machu Picchu! was the immediate recognition as Stephen Tamberly awoke. And then: *No. Not quite. Not as I've known it. When am I?*

He climbed to his feet. Clarity of mind and senses told him he had been knocked out by an electronic stunner, probably a twenty-fourth century model or later. No surprise. The deadly shock had been the apparition of those men on a machine such as was not to be made for thousands of years after he was born.

Around him lifted the peaks he knew, misty, tropically green even at their altitudes save for snow on the most remote. A condor hovered aloft. A blue-and-gold morning flooded the Urubamba gorge with light. But he saw no railway down there, no station, and the only road in sight was up here, built by engineers of the Incas.

He stood on a platform that had been attached, with a descending ramp, to a high point on a wall above a ditch. Below him the city spread over acre upon acre; it clung, it soared, in buildings of dry-laid stone, staircases, terraces, and plazas as powerful as the mountains themselves. If those heights might almost have been from a Chinese painting, the human works might almost have been from medieval southern France; and yet not really, for they were too foreign, too imbued with their own spirit.

A breeze blew cool. Its whittering was the single sound amidst the bloodbeat in his temples. Nothing stirred throughout the fastness. With the mind-speed of desperation, he saw that it had not long lain deserted. Weeds and shrubs were everywhere, but they and the weather had hardly begun the work of demolition. That didn't reveal much, for it still had far to go when Hiram Bingham discovered the place in 1911. However, he spied structures almost intact which he remembered as ruins or not at all. Traces remained of wood and thatch roofs. And—

And Tamberly was not alone. Luis Castelar crouched beside him, stupefaction fading out before a snarl. Men and women stood around, themselves tense. The timecycle rested near the platform edge.

First Tamberly was aware of weapons aimed at him. Then he stared at the people. They were like none he had met in his wanderings. Their very alienness made them look somehow alike. Faces were finely chiseled, high in the cheekbones, thin in the noses, large in the eyes. Despite raven darkness of hair, skin was alabaster and irises were light, while men seemed never to have had any growth of beard. Bodies poised tall, slender, supple. Basic clothing for both sexes was a close-fitted one-piece garment with no visible seams or fastenings and soft half-boots of the same lustrous black. Silver patterns—an Oriental-like tracery—ornamented most, and several persons added cloaks of flamboyant red, orange, or yellow. Wide belts held pockets and holsters. Hair fell to the shoulders and was held in place by a simple headband, arabesqued fillet, or diamond-glittery coronet.

They numbered about thirty. All seemed young—or ageless? Tamberly thought he perceived many years of lifespan behind them. It showed in both the pride and the alertness, above a feline self-composure.

Castelar glared from side to side. He had been deprived of knife and sword. The latter flashed in the hand of a stranger. He tautened as if to attack. Tamberly caught him by the arm. "Peace, Don Luis," he urged. "This is hopeless. Call on the saints if you wish, but stay quiet."

The Spaniard growled before he subsided. Tamberly felt him shiver beneath sleeve and skin. Somebody in the group said something in a language that purred and trilled. Another gestured, as if for silence, and stepped forward. The grace of the motion was such that one could say he flowed. Clearly, he dominated the rest. His features were aquiline, green-eyed. Full lips curved in a smile.

"Greeting," he said. "You are unexpected guests."

He used fluent Temporal, the common speech of the Time Patrol and many civilian travelers; and the machine was scarcely different from a Patrol runabout; but, he must surely be an outlaw, an enemy.

Breath shuddered into Tamberly. "Where is . . . here?" he mumbled. "What year is this?"

Peripherally, he noticed Castelar's reactions when Fray Tanaquil replied in the unknown tongue—astonishment, dismay, grimness.

"By the Gregorian calendar, which I suppose you are accustomed to, it is the fifteenth of April, 1610," said the stranger, "and we are at Vilcabamba."

Of course, passed through Tamberly. *What the natives of Bingham's day called Machu Picchu was once Vilcabamba.* Twentieth-century academic controversies about that gibed at him from the fringes of his mind. *The Inca Pachacutec built it as a holy city, a center for the Virgins of the Sun. Later it became the spiritual headquarters of resistance to the Spaniards, till they captured and killed Tupac Amaru, the last who bore the name of Inca before the Andean Resurgence of the twenty-second century. But the Conquistadores never found Vilcabamba, and it lay empty, forgotten by everyone but a few poor countryfolk, till 1911. . . .* He barely heard: "I suppose, likewise, you are an agent of the Time Patrol."

"Who are *you?*" Tamberly choked.

"Let us discuss matters in a more convenient location," said the man. "This is merely the site to which our scouts returned."

Why? A timecycle could appear within seconds and centimeters of any place, any moment within its range—from here to Earth orbit, from now to the age of the dinosaurs—or, futureward, to the age of the Danellians, though that was forbidden. Tamberly guessed these conspirators built this landing stage, exposed to outside eyes, in order to keep the local Indians frightened and therefore distant. Stories about magical comings and goings would die out in the course of generations, but Machu Picchu would remain shunned.

Most of those who had been watching dispersed to whatever their business was. Four guards with drawn stunners walked behind the leader and prisoners. One also carried the sword, perhaps as a souvenir. By ramp, paths, and staircases they made their way down among the compounds of the city. Silence lay thick about them until the chieftain said, "Apparently your companion is just a soldier who happened to be with you." At the American's nod: "Well, then, we'll put him aside while you and I talk. Yaron, Sarnir, you know his language. Interrogate him. Psychological means only, for the time being."

They had reached that structure which Tamberly, if he remembered aright, knew as the King's Group. An outer wall marked off a small courtyard where another timecycle was parked. Curtains of nacreous iridescence shimmered in doorways and across the roofless tops of the buildings that bounded the rest of the open space. Those were forcefields, Tamberly recognized, impervious to anything short of a nuclear blast.

"In God's name," Castelar cried when a boot nudged him, "what is this? Tell me before I go mad!"

"Easy, Don Luis, easy," Tamberly answered fast. "We're captives. You've seen what their weapons can do. Go as they command. Heaven may have mercy on us, but by ourselves we're helpless."

The Spaniard clenched his jaws and went with the two assigned him, into a lesser unit. The leader's group sought the largest. Barriers blinked out of existence to admit both parties. They stayed off, giving a look at stones and sky and freedom. Tamberly supposed that was to let fresh air in; the room he entered did not appear to have been used lately.

Sunshine joined radiance from the canopy overhead to illuminate its windowlessness. The floor had been given a deep blue covering that responded slightly to footfalls, like living muscles. A couple of chairs and a table bore halfway familiar shapes, though their darkly glowing material was new to him. He could not identify the things shelved in what might have been a cabinet.

The guards took stance on either side of the entrance. One was male, one a woman no less steely. The leader settled into a chair and invited Tamberly to take the other. It fitted itself to his contours, to his every motion. The leader pointed at a carafe and glasses on the table. Those were enameled—made in Venice about now, Tamberly judged. Bought? Stolen? Looted? The man glided forward to fill two vessels. His master and Tamberly took them.

Smiling, the leader lifted his goblet and murmured, "Your health." The implication was: *You'd better do whatever is necessary to keep it.* The wine was a tart chablis type, so refreshing that Tamberly thought it might contain a stimulant. They had broad and subtle knowledge of human chemistry in his future.

"Well, then," the leader said. His tone continued mild. "You are obviously of the Patrol. That was a holographic recorder in your hand. And the Patrol would never permit any visitor out of time to prowl about a moment so critical, except its own."

Tamberly's throat contracted. His tongue stiffened. It was the block laid in his mind during his training, a reflex to keep him from revealing to any unauthorized person, ever, that traffic went up and down the tiers of history. "Uh, uh—I—" Sweat sprang forth cold upon his skin.

"My sympathies." Did laughter run through the words? "I am quite aware of your conditioning. I also realize that it operates within the bounds of common sense. We being time travelers, you are free to discuss that subject, if not those details the Patrol prefers to keep secret. Will it help if I introduce myself? Merau Varagan. If you have heard of my race, it is probably under the name of Exaltationists."

Tamberly recalled enough to make this an hour of nightmare. *The thirty-first millennium was—is—will be—only Temporal grammar has the verbs and tenses to deal with these concepts—it is far earlier than the development of the first time machines, but chosen members of its civilization know about the travel, take part in it, some join the Patrol, like individuals in most milieus. Only . . . this era had its supermen, their genes created for adventurousness on the space frontier; and they came to chafe beneath the weight of that civilization of theirs, which to them was older than the Stone Age is to me; and they rebelled, and lost, and must flee; but they had learned the great fact, that timefaring exists, and had, incredibly, managed to seize some vehicles; and "since then" the Patrol has been on their track, lest they do worse mischief, but I know of no report that the Patrol "will" catch them. . . .*

"I can't tell you more than you've deduced," he protested. "If you torture me to death, I can't."

"When a man plays a dangerous game," replied Merau Varagan, "he should prepare contingencies. I admit we failed to anticipate your presence. We thought the treasure vault would be deserted at night, except for sentries outside. However, the possibility of an encounter with the Patrol has been very much on our minds. Raor, the kyradex."

Before Tamberly could wonder what that word meant, the woman was at his side. Horror surged through him as he divined her purpose. He started to rise, scramble free, get himself killed, anything.

Her pistol blinked. It was set to less than knockout force. His sinews gave way, he flopped back onto his chair. Only its embrace kept him for sliding to the carpet.

She sought the cabinet, returned with an object.

It was a box and a sort of luminous helmet, joined by a cable. The hemisphere went over his head. Raor's fingers danced across glow-spots that must be controls. Symbols appeared in the air. Meter readings? A humming took hold of Tamberly. It grew and grew until it was all there was, he was lost in it, he spun down into the darkness at its heart.

Slowly he ascended. He regained use of his muscles and straightened in the seat. Relaxation pervaded him, though, like that which follows long sleep. He seemed detached from himself, an observer outside, emotionless. Yet he was totally awake. Every sensory detail stood forth, smells of his unwashed robe and body, mountain air coming sharp through the doorway, Varagan's sardonic Caesar visage, Raor with the box in her hand, the weight of the helmet, a fly that sat on the wall as if to remind him he was as mortal as it.

Varagan leaned back, crossed his legs, bridged his fingers, and said with weird courtesy, "Your name and origin, please."

"Stephen John Tamberly. Born in San Francisco, California, United States of America, June the twenty-third, 1937."

He answered fully and truthfully. He must. Or, rather, his memory, nerves, mouth must. The kyradex was the ultimate interrogator. He could not even feel the ghastliness of his condition. Deep underneath, something screamed, but his conscious mind had become a machine.

"And when were you recruited into the Patrol?"

"In 1968." It had happened too gradually for him to give an exact date. A colleague introduced him to some friends, interesting sorts who, he understood afterward, sounded him out; eventually he agreed to take certain tests, allegedly as part of a psychological research project; afterward the situation was revealed to him; he was invited to enlist, and accepted with infinite eagerness, as they had known he would. Well, he was on the rebound from divorce. The decision would have been more difficult if he'd had to lead a double life constantly. Regardless, he knew he would have, for it gave him worlds to explore that until then had been only writings, ruins, shards, and dead bones.

"What is your standing in the organization?"

"I'm not in enforcement or rescue or anything of that sort. I'm a field historian. At home I was an anthropologist, had done work among the modern Quechua, then went into the archaeology of the region. That made me a natural choice for the Conquest period. I would have liked better to study the pre-Columbian societies, but of course that was impossible; I'd have been too conspicuous."

"I see. How long is your Patrol career thus far?"

"About sixty years of lifespan." You could run up centuries, doubling around in time. A tremendous perquisite of membership was the longevity process of an era futureward of his own. To be sure, that brought the pain of watching people you loved grow old and die, never knowing what you knew. To escape that, as a general thing you phased out of their lives, let them believe you'd moved away, made contact with them dwindle gradually to nothing. For they must not notice how the years did not gnaw you down like them.

"Where and when did you depart on this latest mission of yours?"

"From California in 1968." He had maintained his old relationships longer than most agents did. His lifespan age might be ninety, his biological age thirty, but stress and sorrow told on a man, and in 1986 he could claim his calendrical age of fifty, though kinfolk often remarked how youthful he still looked. God knew there was grief aplenty in a Patrolman's days, along with the adventure. You witnessed too much.

"Hm," said Varagan. "We'll go into that in more detail. First describe your assignment. Just what were you doing last century in Cajamarca?"

The later name of the town, observed a distant part of Tamberly, while his automaton consciousness replied: "I told you, I'm a field historian, gathering data on the period of the Conquest." It was for more than the sake of science. How could the Patrol police the time lanes and maintain the reality of events unless it knew what those events were? Books were often misleading, and many a key happening was never chronicled. "The corps got me accredited—as Estebán Tanaquil, a Franciscan friar—accredited to Pizarro's expedition when he returned in 1530 from Spain to America." —before Waldseemüller bestowed that name. "I was simply to observe, recording as much as I was able unbeknownst." And do what heartbreakingly slight things he could to lighten, the tiniest bit, the brutality. "You must know, too, those years will loom large in history—futureward of my home century, pastward of yours—when the Resurgents call on their Andean heritage."

Varagan nodded. "Indeed," he said conversationally. "If matters had gone otherwise, why, already the twentieth century might be very different." He grinned. "Suppose, for example, Inca Huayna Capac had not divided heirship between his sons Huáscar and Atahuallpa. Then the empire would not have been in a state of civil war when Pizzaro arrived. His minuscule gang of adventurers could not possibly have overthrown it. The Conquest would have required more time, more resources. This would have affected the balance of power in Europe, where the Turks were pressing inward while the Reformation broke what scant unity Christendom had possessed."

"Is that your aim?" In vague way Tamberly knew he should be furious, aghast, anything but apathetic. He barely had the curiosity to ask the question.

"Perhaps," Varagan taunted. "However, the men who found you were only scouts in advance of a much more modest enterprise, bringing Atahuallpa's ransom here. That would be quite upsetting in itself, of course." He laughed. "But it might preserve those priceless works of art. You were content to make holograms of them for people uptime."

"For all humankind," said Tamberly automatically.

41

"Well, for such of it as can be allowed to enjoy the fruits of time travel, under the watchful eye of the Patrol."

"Bring the treasure . . . here?" fumbled Tamberly. "Now?"

"Temporarily. We've camped where we are because it's a convenient base." Varagan scowled. "The Patrol is too vigilant in our original milieu. Arrogant swine!" Calm again: "As isolated as Vilcabamba is at present, it will not be noticeably affected by changes in the near past—for instance, by such a detail as Atahuallpa's ransom unaccountably disappearing one night. But your associates will be in full quest of you, Tamberly. They'll follow up every last clue they can find. Best we have that information at once, to forestall any moves of theirs."

I should be shaken to the roots of my soul. This utter, absolute recklessness—risking loops in the world lines, temporal vortices, destruction of the whole future. No, not risking. Deliberately bringing it about. But I cannot feel the horror. The thing that squats on my skull holds down my humanity.

Varagan leaned forward. "Therefore let us discuss your personal history," he said. "What do you consider your home? What family have you, friends, ties of any kind?"

The questions quickly became knife-sharp. Tamberly watched and listened while their skilled wielder cut from him detail after detail. When something especially interested Varagan, he pursued it to the end. Tamberly's second wife ought to be safe; she was also in the Patrol. His first wife was remarried, out of his life. But oh, God, his brother, and Bill's own wife, and he heard himself confess that his niece was like a daughter to him—

The doorway darkened. Luis Castelar bounded through.

His sword slashed. The guard there buckled, crumpled, fell and lay squirming. Blood spouted from his throat, its red like the shriek he could no longer sound forth.

Raor dropped the control box and snatched for her sidearm. Castelar reached her. His left fist smashed at her jaw. She staggered back, sagged, went to the floor and gaped up at him, stunned. His blade sang even as she dropped. Varagan was on his feet. Incredibly quick, he dodged a cut that would have laid him open. The room was too cramped for him to get past. Castelar stabbed. Varagan clutched his belly. Blood squirted between his fingers. He leaned against the wall and shouted.

Castelar wasted no time finishing him. The

Spaniard ripped the helmet off Tamberly. It thudded to the floor. Wholeness of spirit broke like a sunbeam into the American.

"Get us away!" Castelar rasped. "The witch-horse outside—"

Tamberly reeled from his chair. His knees would barely hold him. Castelar's free arm gave support. They stumbled into the open. The time-cycle waited. Tamberly crawled onto the front saddle, Castlar leaped to the rear. A man in black appeared in the courtyard gateway. He yelled and reached for his weapon.

Tamberly slapped the console.

11 MAY 2937 B.C.

Machu Picchu was gone. Wind surrounded him. Hundreds of feet below lay a river valley, lush with grass and groves. Ocean gleamed in the distance.

The cycle dropped. Air brawled. Tamberly's hands sought the gravity drive. The engine awoke. The fall stopped. He brought the vehicle to a smooth and silent landing.

He began to shake. Darkness went in rags before his eyes.

The reaction passed. He grew aware of Castelar standing on the ground beside him, and the Spaniard's swordpoint an inch from his throat.

"Get off that thing," Castelar said. "Move carefully, your arms up. You are no holy man. I think you may be a magician who should burn at the stake. We will find out."

3 NOVEMBER 1885

A hansom cab brought Manse Everard from Dalhousie & Roberts, Importers—which was also the Time Patrol's London base in this milieu—to the house on York Place. He mounted the stairs through a dense yellowish fog and turned the handle on a doorbell. A maidservant let him into a wainscoted anteroom. He gave her a card. She was back in a minute to say that Mrs. Tamberly would be pleased to receive him. He left his hat and overcoat on a rack and followed her. Interior heating failed to keep out all the dank chill, which made him for once glad to be dressed like a Victorian gentleman. Usually he found such clothes abominably uncomfortable. Otherwise this was, on the whole, a marvelous era to live in, if you had money, enjoyed robust health, and could pass for an Anglo-Saxon Protestant.

The parlor was a pleasant, gas-lit room, lined with books and not overly cluttered with bric-a-brac. A coal fire burned low. Helen Tamberly stood close, as if in need of what cheer it offered. She was a small reddish-blond woman; the full dress subtly emphasized a figure that many doubtless envied. Her voice made the Queen's English musical. It wavered a little, though. "How do you do, Mr. Everard. Please be seated. Would you care for tea?"

"No, thanks, ma'am unless you want some." He made no effort to dissemble his American accent. "Another man is due here shortly. Maybe after we've talked with him?"

"Certainly." She nodded dismissal to the maid,

who left the door open behind her. Helen Tamberly went to close it. "I hope this doesn't shock Jenkins too badly," she said with a wan smile.

"I daresay she's grown used to somewhat unconventional ways around here," Everard responded in an effort to match her self-possession.

"Well, we try not to be too outré. People tolerate a certain amount of eccentricity. If our front were upper class, rather than well-to-do bourgeois, we could get away with anything; but then we'd be too much in the public eye." She stepped across the carpet to stand before him, fists clenched at her sides. "Enough of that," she said desperately. "You're from the Patrol. An Unattached agent, am I right? It's about Stephen. Must be. Tell me."

Without fear of eavesdroppers, he continued in the English language, which might sound gentler in her ears than Temporal. "Yes. Now we don't yet know anything for sure. He's—missing. Failed to report in. I suppose you remember that was to have been in Lima late in 1535, several months after Pizarro founded it. We have an outpost there. Discreet inquiries turned up the fact that the friar Estebán Tanaquil vanished mysteriously two years before, in Cajamarca. Vanished, mind you, not died in some accident or affray or whatever." Bleakly: "Nothing as simple as that."

"But he could be alive?" she cried.

"We may hope. I can't promise more than that the Patrol will try its damnedest—uh, pardon me."

She gave a broken laugh. "That's all right. If you're from Stephen's milieu, everybody's careless with speech, true?"

"Well, he and I were both born and raised in the U.S.A., middle twentieth century. That's why I've been asked to lead this investigation. A background shared with your husband just might give me some useful insight."

"You were asked," she murmured. "Nobody gives orders to an Unattached agent, nobody less than a Danellian."

"That's not quite correct," he said awkwardly. Sometimes his status—assigned to no particular milieu, but free to go anywhere and anywhen there was need and act on his own judgment—embarrassed him. He was by nature unpretentious, a meat-and-potatoes kind of man.

"Good of you to agree," she said and blinked hard against tears. "Do please be seated. Smoke if you wish. Are you quite sure you wouldn't care for tea and biscuits or perhaps a spot of brandy?"

"Maybe later, thanks. But I will avail myself of my pipe." He waited till she sat down by the hearth to take the armchair opposite, which must be Steve Tamberly's. The fire quivered blue between them.

"I've been in on a few cases like this in the past—my lifeline past, that is," he began cautiously. "It's desirable to start by learning as much as possible about the person concerned. That means talking with those close to him or her. So I've come a tad early today, hoping we could get acquainted. An agent who's been on the spot will be along in a while to tell us what he discovered. I assumed you wouldn't mind."

"Oh, no." She drew breath. "But tell me, please. I've always had difficulty understanding, even when I think in Temporal. My father was a physics don, and it's hard to set aside the strict logic of cause and effect he drilled into me. Stephen . . . encountered trouble somehow, in sixteenth-century Perú. Maybe the Patrol can save him, maybe it can't. Whatever, though, whatever the result is . . . the Patrol will know. There'll be a report in the files. Can't you go at once and read it? Or, or skip ahead in time and ask your future self? Why must we go through *this*?"

Upbringing or no, she must be hideously shaken to raise such a question, she who had also been trained at that academy back in the Oligocene period—back before there was any human history for its existence to upset. Everard didn't think the less of her. Rather, it made him appreciate the courage that maintained her calmness. And, after all, her work did not expose her to the paradoxes and hazards of mutable time. Nor had Tamberly experienced them—he had been a straightforward, if disguised, observer—till suddenly they laid hold of him.

"You know that's forbidden." He kept his tone soft. "Causal loops can too easily turn into temporal vortices. Annulment of the whole effort would be the least of the disasters we'd risk. And it'd be futile, anyway. Those records, those memories could be of something that never happened. Just think how our actions would be influenced by what we believed was foreknowledge. No, we've got to go through with our jobs in as nearly causal a way as we possibly can, in order to *make* our successes or failures real."

For reality is conditional. It is like a wave pattern on a sea. Let the waves—the probability-waves of ultimate underlying quantum chaos—change their rhythm, and abruptly that tracery of ripples and foam-swirls will be gone, transformed into another. Already in the twentieth century, physicists had a dim glimmering of this. But not until time travel came to be did the fact of it stab into human lives.

If you have gone into the past, you have made it your present. You have the same free will as always. You have laid no special constraints on yourself. Inevitably, you influence what happens.

Ordinarily the effects are slight. It's as if the space-time continuum was like a mesh of tough rubber bands, restoring its configuration after it's felt some disturbing force. Indeed, ordinarily you are a part of the past. There really was a man who traveled with Pizarro and called himself Brother Tanaquil. That was "always" true, and the fact that he wasn't born in that century, but long afterward, is incidental. If he does minor anachronistic things, they don't matter; they may excite comment, but memory of them will die out. It's a philosophical question whether or not reality keeps flickering through such insignificant changes.

Some acts, though, do make a difference. What if a lunatic went back to the fifth century and provided Attila the Hun with machine guns? That kind of thing is so obvious it's fairly easy to guard against. But subtler **5 8** *changes—the Bolshevik Revolution of 1917 came near to failing. Only the energy and genius of Lenin pulled it through. What if you traveled to the nineteenth century and quietly, harmlessly prevented Lenin's parents from ever meeting each other? Whatever else the Russian Empire later became, it would not be the Soviet Union, and the consequences of that would pervade all history afterward. You, pastward of the change, would still be there; but returning futureward, you'd find a totally different world, a world in which you yourself were probably never born. You'd exist, but as an effect without a cause, thrown up into existence by that anarchy which is at its foundation.*

When the first time machine had been built, the Danellians appeared, the superhumans who inhabit the remote future. They ordained the rules of time traffic and established the Patrol to enforce these. Like other police, we mostly assist people on their lawful occasions; we get them out of tight spots when we can; we give what help and kindness we dare to the victims of history. But always our basic mission is to protect and preserve that history, because it is what shall finally bring forth the glorious Danellians.

"I'm sorry," Helen Tamberly said. "That was

idiotic of me. But I've been . . . so worried. Stephen was only supposed to be gone three days. Six years for him, three days for me. He wanted that much time merely to reaccustom himself to this milieu. He meant to wander about incognito, getting back into Victorian habits, so he wouldn't absent-mindedly do something that would surprise the servants or our local friends. It's been a week !" She bit her lip. "Forgive me. I'm still babbling, am I not?"

"Far from it." Everard took forth pipe and tobacco pouch. He wanted that small comfort in the face of this anguish. "Loving couples like you make a bachelor like me feel wistful. But let's get down to business. Best for us both. You're native to England of this century, aren't you?"

She nodded. "Born in Cambridge, 1856. I was orphaned at seventeen, left with modest independent means, studied classics, became rather a bluestocking, eventually was recruited into the Patrol. Stephen and I met at the Academy. In spite of the age difference—which doesn't matter for us, thank God—we hit it off, and married after we graduated. He didn't think I would like his birthtime." She grimaced. "I visited it, and he was right. For his part, he felt—feels happy here and now. His persona is that of an American employee of the import firm. When I go off to my own work, or bring some home with me, well, it is unusual for a woman to have sholarly interests, but not extraordinary. Marie Sklodowska—Madame Curie—will enroll in the Sorbonne just a few years hence."

"And people in this milieu are better at minding their own affairs than they are in mine." Everard occupied himself with tamping his briar full. "Uh, I daresay you two do more things together than is common for man and wife these days."

"Oh, yes." Her eagerness was pathetic to hear. "Beginnning with our holidays, in this era and that. We fell quite in love with archaic Japan, and have been back several times." Everard concluded that that was a country isolated enough, with a population small and unsophisticated enough, illiterate enough, that the Patrol allowed occasional visits by blatant outsiders. "We've taken up handicrafts; pottery, for example; that ashtray beside you is his work—" Her voice died away.

Hastily, he queried onward. "Your field is ancient Greece?" The man who met him at the base hadn't been sure.

"The Ionian colonies, chiefly in the seventh and sixth centuries before Christ." She sighed. "It's ironic that there the Patrol cannot admit me, a Nordic woman." She tried to rally. "But as I said, we've seen much else that is wonderful." Suitably outfitted, carefully guided. "No, I mustn't complain." The stoicism cracked. "If Stephen—if you do bring him back—do you think he can be persuaded to settle down and do research in place, like me?"

Everard's match cast a loud *scrit* across the silence that followed. He rolled smoke over his tongue and cradled the rough wood in his hand. "Don't count on it," he said. "Besides, good field historians are scarce. Good people of every kind are. You may not be fully aware of how undermanned we are in the corps. Your sort make it possible for his sort to operate. And mine. Normally we come home safe."

Patrol work was anything but bravado and derring-do. It depended on exact knowledge. Agents like Steve collected most of that on the spot, but they too required the patient labor of those like Helen, who collated the reports. Thus, observers in Ionia brought back immensely more information that those chronicles and relics that survived into the nineteenth century had ever contained; but they could not do her job, which was to put it all together, interpret, arrange, and prepare briefings for the next expeditions.

"Someday he must find something safer." She blushed. "I refuse to start a family until he does."

"Oh, I'm sure he'll move into an administrative post in due course," Everard answered. *If we can save him.* "He'll have gotten far too much experience for us to let him go on grubbing around. Instead, he'll direct the efforts of newer people. Um, that may well require his assuming a Spanish colonial persona for a few decades. It'd be easiest if you could join him."

"What an adventure! I should adapt. We didn't plan on remaining Victorians forever."

"And you've ruled out twentieth-century America. Hm, what about his ties there?"

"He comes from an old California family. It has

distant Peruvian connections. A great-grandfather of his was a sea captain who married a young lady in Lima and brought her home with him. Perhaps that helped interest him in early Perú. I suppose you know he became an anthropologist and later practiced archaeology down there. He has a married brother in San Francisco. His own first marriage ended in divorce, shortly before he enlisted in the Patrol. That was—will be—in 1968. Subsequently he resigned his professorship and told everyone he had a grant from a learned institution, which would enable him to do independent research. This explains his frequent prolonged absences. He does still keep bachelor quarters, so as to remain in touch with kin and friends, and has no plans at present to phase out of their lives. At last he must, and knows it, but—" She smiled. "He has talked about seeing his favorite niece get married and have a baby. He says he wants to enjoy being a granduncle."

Everard ignored the scrambled tenses. It was inevitable when you spoke any language but Temporal. "Favorite niece, eh?" he murmured. "That kind of person is often useful, apt to know a lot and tell it freely without getting suspicious. What do you know about her?"

"Her name is Wanda, and she was born in 1965. The last several mentions of her that Stephen made to me, she was, m-m, a student of biology at a place called Stanford University. As a matter of fact, he scheduled his departure on this last mission from

California rather than London so he could first see his relatives there in, oh, yes, 1986."

"I had better interview her."

A knock sounded on the door. "Come in," the woman called.

The maid entered. "There is a person who asks to see you, Missus," she announced. "Mr. Basscase, he says is his name." With frosty disapproval: "A gentlemen of color."

"That's the other agent," Everard muttered to his hostess. "Earlier than I expected."

"Send him in," she directed.

Julio Vasquez did indeed look out of place: short, stocky, bronze of skin, black of hair, with wide features and an arched nose. He was almost pure native Andean, though born in the twenty-second century, Everard knew. Still, this neighborhood had doubtless grown somewhat accustomed to exotic visitors. Not only was London the center of a planetwide empire, York Place divided Baker Street.

Helen Tamberly received the newcomer graciously, and now she did send for tea. The Patrol had cured her of any Victorian racism. Necessarily, the language became Temporal, for she knew no Spanish (or Quechua!) and English was not important enough in his life, either before or after he joined the Patrol, for him to acquire more that some stock phrases.

"I have learned very little," he said. "It was an

especially difficult undertaking, the more so on such
short notice. To the Spaniards I was merely another
Indian. How could I approach one, let alone make
inquiries of him? I could have been flogged for
insolence, or killed out of hand."

"The Conquistadores were a bunch of bas—of
hellhounds, all right," Everard remarked. "As I recall, after Atahuallpa's ransom was in, Pizarro didn't
let him go. No, he put him before a kangaroo court
on a bunch of trumped-up charges and sentenced
him to death. To be burned alive, wasn't it?"

"It was commuted to strangling when he accepted baptism," Vasquez said, "and a number of
the Spanish, including Pizarro himself, felt guilty
about the matter afterward. They had been afraid
Atahuallpa, set free, would stir up a revolt against
them. Their later puppet Inca, Manco, did." He
paused. "Yes, the Conquest was ghastly, slaughters,
lootings, enslavements. But, my friends, you were
taught history in anglophone schools, and Spain
was for centuries England's rival. Propaganda from
that conflict has endured. The truth is that the
Spaniards, Inquisition and all, were no worse than
anyone else of that era, and better than many.
Some, such as Cortés himself, and even Torque-
mada, tried to get a measure of justice for the
natives. It is worth remembering that those popula-
tions survived throughout most of Latin America,
on ancestral soil, whereas the English, with their
Yanqui and Canadian successors, made a nearly
clean sweep."

"Touché," said Everard wryly.

"Please," Helen Tamberly whispered.

"My apologies, *señora*." Vasquez gave her a bow from his chair. "I did not mean to tantalize you, only to explain why I could find out very little. Apparently the friar and soldier went into the house where the hoard was kept one night. When they did not reappear by dawn, the guards grew nervous and opened the door. They were not inside. Every door had been watched. Sensational rumors flew. What I heard was through the Indios, and I could not query them, either. Remember, I was a stranger among them, and they hardly ever traveled away from home. The upheaval in progress allowed me to concoct a story accounting for my presence in the city, but it would not have withstood examination, had anyone grown interested in me."

Everard puffed hard on his pipe. "Hm," he said around it, "I gather that Tamberly, as the friar, had access to each new load of treasure, to pray over it or whatever. Actually, he took holograms of the artwork, for future people's information and enjoyment. But what about that soldier?"

Vasquez shrugged. "I heard his name, Luis Castelar, and that he was a cavalry officer who had distinguished himself in the campaign. Some said he might have plotted to steal the wealth, but others replied that that was unthinkable of so honorable a knight, not to mention good-hearted Fray Tanaquil. Pizarro interrogated the sentries at length but, I heard, satisfied himself about their honesty. After all, the hoard was still there. When I left, the general idea was that sorcerers had been at work. Hysteria was building rapidly. It could have hideous consequences."

"Which are *not* in the history we learned," Everard growled. "How critical is that exact piece of space-time?"

66   "The Conquest as a whole, certainly vital, a key part of world events. This one episode—who knows? We have not ceased to exist, in spite of being uptime of it."

"Which doesn't mean we can't cease," said Everard roughly. *We can have never been, ourselves and the whole world that begot us. It's a perishing more absolute than death.* "The Patrol shall concentrate everything it can spare on that span of days or weeks. And proceed with extreme caution," he added to Helen Tamberly. "What could have happened? Have you any clues, Agent Vasquez?"

"I may have a slender one," the other man told them. "I suspect that somebody with a time vehicle had in mind hijacking the ransom."

"Yeah, that's a fair guess. One of Tamberly's assignments was to keep an eye on developments and let the Patrol know of anything suspicious."

"How could he before he returned uptime?" the woman wondered.

"He left recorded messages in what looked like ordinary rocks, but which emitted identifying Y-radiation," Everard explained. "The agreed-on spots were checked, but nothing was there except brief, routine reports on what he'd been experiencing."

"I was taken from my real mission for this investigation," Vasquez went on. "My work was a generation earlier, in the reign of Huayna Capac, father of Atahuallpla and Huáscar. We can't understand the Conquest without an understanding of the great and complex civilization that it destroyed." 6 7 An imperium reaching from Ecuador deep into Chile, and from the Pacific seaboard to the headwaters of the Amazon. "And . . . it seems that strangers appeared at the court of Inca in 1524, about a year before his death. They resembled Europeans and were taken to be such; the realm had heard rumors of men from afar. They left after a while, nobody knew where or how. But when I was called back uptime, I had begun to get intimations that they tried to persuade Huayna not to bequeath a split power to his sons. They failed; the old man was stubborn. But that the attempt was made is significant, no?"

Everard whistled. "God, yes! Did you get any hint as to who those visitors might have been?"

"No. Nothing worthwhile. That entire milieu is exceptionally hard to penetrate." Vasquez made a crooked smile. "Having defended the Spaniards against the charge of having been monsters, by sixteenth-century standards, I must say that the Inca state was not a nation of peaceful innocents. It was aggressively expanding in every possible direction.

And it was totalitarian; it regulated life down to the last detail. Not unkindly; if you conformed, you were provided for. But woe betide you if you did not. The very nobles lacked any freedom worth mentioning. Only the Inca, the god-king, had that. You can see the difficulties an outsider confronts, regardless of whether he belongs to the same race. In Caxamalca I said I had been sent to report on my district to the bureaucracy. Before Pizarro upset the reign, I could never have made that story stick. As it was, all I got to hear was second- and third-hand gossip."

Everard nodded. Like practically everything in history, the Spanish Conquest was neither entirely bad nor entirely good. Cortés at least put an end to the grisly massacre-sacrifices of the Aztecs, and Pizzaro opened the way for a concept of individual dignity and worth. Both invaders had Indian allies, who joined them for excellent reasons.

Well, a Patrolman had no business moralizing. His duty was to preserve what *was*, from end to end of time, and to stand by his comrades.

"Let's talk about whatever we can think of that might conceivably be of help," he proposed. "Mrs. Tamberly, we will not abandon your husband to his fate. Maybe we can't rescue him, but we're sure going to give it our best try."

Jenkins brought in tea.

30 OCTOBER 1986

Mr. Everard is a surprise. His letters and then his phone calls from New York were, well, polite and kind of intellectual. Here he is in person, a big bruiser with a dented nose. How old is he, forty? Hard to tell. I'm sure he's knocked around a lot.

No matter his looks. (They could be mighty sexy if things took that turn. Which they won't. Doubtless for the best, damn it.) He's soft-spoken, with the same old-fashioned quality his communications had.

Shake hands. "Glad to meet you, Miss Tamberly," the deep voice says. "It's kind of you to come here." Downtown hotel, the lobby.

"Well, it concerns my one and only uncle, doesn't it?" I toss back.

He nods. "I'd like to speak with you at length. Uh, would it be forward of me if I offered to stand you a drink? Or dinner? I'll be putting you to certain amount of trouble."

Caution. "Thanks, but let'see how it goes. Right now, frankly, I'm too keyed up. Could we just walk for a while?"

"Why not? A beautiful day, and I haven't been in Palo Alto in years. Maybe we can go to the university and stroll around?"

Gorgeous weather for sure, Indian summer before the rains start in earnest. If it lasts we'll have smog. Right now, clear blue overhead, sunlight spilling down like a waterfall. The eucalyptuses on campus will be all silvery and pale green and pungent. In spite of the situation (oh, what has become of Uncle Steve?) I can't keep excitement down. Me, with a real live detective.

Turn left in the street. "What do you want, Mr. Everard?"

"To interview you exactly as I told you. I'd like to draw you out about Dr. Tamberly. Something you say might give an inkling."

Good of that foundation to care, to hire this man. Well, naturally, they have an investment in Uncle Steve. He's doing that research down in South America that he's never talked much about. Must be one dynamite book he means to write. Reflect credit on the foundation. Help justify its tax exemption. No, I shouldn't think that. Cheap cynicism is for sophomores.

"Why me, though? I mean, my dad's his brother. He'd know a lot more."

"Maybe. I do intend to see him and his wife. But the information given me says you're a special favorite of your uncle's. I've got a hunch he's revealed things about himself to you—nothing big, nothing you imagine is very special—but things that might give some insight into his character, some clue as to where he went."

Swallow hard. Six months, now, with never so much as a postcard. "Have they no idea at the foundation?"

"You asked me before," Everard reminds. "He always was an independent operator. Made it a condition of accepting the funds. Yes, he was bound for the Andes, but we hadly know more than that. It's a huge territory. The police authorities of the several possible countries haven't been able to tell us a thing."

This is hard to say. Melodrama. But. "Do you suspect . . . foul play?"

"We don't know, Miss Tamberly. We hope not. Maybe he took too long a chance and—Anyway, my job's to try understanding him." He smiles. It creases his face. "My notion of how to do that is to start by understanding the people he feels close to."

"He always was, you know, reserved. Quite a private guy."

"With a soft spot for you, however. Mind if I ask you a few questions about yourself, for openers?"

"Go ahead. I don't guarantee to answer them all."

"Nothing too personal. Let's see. You're in your senior year at Stanford, right? What's your major?"

"Biology."

"That's about as broad a word as 'physics,' isn't it?"

He's no dummy. "Well, I'm mainly interested in evolutionary transitions. Probably I'll go into paleontology."

"You plan on grad school, then?"

"Oh, yes. A Ph.D.'s the union card if you want to do science."

"You look more athletic than academic, if I may say so."

"Tennis, backpacking, sure, I like it outdoors, and fossicking for fossils is a great way to get paid for being there." Impulse. "I've got a summer job lined up. Tourist guide in the Galápagos Islands. The Lost World if ever there was a Lost World." Suddenly my eyes sting and blur. "Uncle Steve arranged it for me. He has friends in Ecuador."

"Sounds terrific. How's your Spanish?"

"Pretty good. We, my family, used to vacation a lot in México. I still go now and then, and I've traveled in South America."

—He's been remarkably easy to talk with. "Comfortable as an old shoe," Dad would say. We sat on a campus bench, we had a beer in the union, he did end up taking me to dinner. Nothing fancy, nothing romantic. But worth cutting those classes for. I've told him an awful lot.

Funny how little he's managed to tell about himself.

I realize that as he says goodnight outside my apartment building. "You've been most helpful, Miss Tamberly. Maybe more than you know. I'll get hold of your parents tomorrow. Then back to New York, I suppose. Here." He takes out his wallet, extracts a small white oblong. "My card. If anything else should come to your mind, please phone me at once, collect." Dead seriousness: "Or if anything happens that seems the least peculiar. Please. This might be a tad dangerous, this business."

Uncle Steve involved with the C.I.A, or what? Suddenly the evening doesn't feel mild. "Okay. Goodnight, Mr. Everard." I snatch the card and hurry through the door.

11 MAY 2937 B.C.

"When I saw they were off guard and close together," Castelar said, "I called on Sant'Iago in my mind, and sprang. My kick took the first in the throat and he went to the floor. I whirled about and gave the second the heel of my hand below the nose, an upward blow, *thus.*" The movement was quick and savage. "He fell, too. I retrieved my blade, made sure of them both, and came after you."

His tone was almost casual. Tamberly thought, in the daze dulling his brain, that the Exaltationists had made the common mistake of underestimating a man of a past era. This one was ignorant of nearly everything they knew, but his wits were fully equal to theirs. Thereon was laid a ferocity bred by centuries of war—not impersonal high-technological conflict but medieval combat, where you looked into your enemy's eyes and cut him down with your own hand.

"Were you not the least afraid of their . . . magic?" Tamberly mumbled.

Castelar shook his head. "I knew God was with me." He crossed himself, then sighed. "It was stupid of me to leave their guns behind. I will not fail like that again."

Despite the heat, Tamberly shivered.

He sat slumped in long grass beneath a noonday sun. Castelar stood above him, metal shining, hand on hilt, legs apart, like a colossus bestriding the world. The timecycle rested several yards off. Beyond, a stream flowed toward the sea, which was

not visible here but which he estimated, from his
glimpse aloft, lay twenty or thirty miles distant.
Palm, chirimoya, and other vegetation told him they
were "still" in tropical America. He had a vague
recollection of chancing to give the temporal activator a harder thrust than the spatial.

Could he get up, make a break for it, beat the
Spaniard to the machine and escape? Impossible.
Were he in better shape, he would try. Like most
field agents, he'd received training in martial arts.
That might offset the other's cruder skills and
greater strength. (Any cavalier spent his whole life
in such physical activity that an Olympic champion
would be flabby by comparison.) Now he was too
weak, in body and mind alike. With the kyradex off
his head, he had volition again. But it wasn't much
use yet. He felt drained, sand in his synapses, lead
in his eyelids, skull scooped hollow.

Castelar glowered downward. "Cease twisting
words, sorcerer," he rapped. "It is for me to put
you to the question."

*Should I just keep mum and provoke him into killing
me?* Tamberly wondered in his weariness. *I imagine
he'd apply torture first, seeking to force my cooperation.
But afterward he'd be stranded, made harmless. . . . No.
He'd be sure to monkey with the vehicle. That could easily
bring about his destruction; but if it didn't, what else
could happen? I must keep my death in reserve till I'm
certain it's the only thing I have to offer.*

He lifted his gaze to the dark eagle visage and

dragged forth: "I am no sorcerer. I merely have knowledge you don't, of various arts and devices. The Indios thought our musketeers commanded the lightning. It was simple gunpowder. A compass needle points north, but not by magic." *Though you don't understand the actual principle, do you?* "Likewise for weapons that stun without wounding, and for engines that overleap space and time"

Castelar nodded. "I had that feeling," he said slowly. "My captors whom I slew let words drop."

Lord, this is a bright fellow! A genius, perhaps, in his fashion. Yes, I remember him remarking that besides his studies among the priests, he's enjoyed reading stories of Amadis—those fantastic romances that inflamed the imagination of his era—and another remark once showed a surprisingly sophisticated view of Islam.

Castelar tautened. "Then tell me what this is about," he demanded. "What are you in truth, you who falsely claim ordainment?"

Tamberly groped through his mind. No barriers crossed it. The kyradex had wiped out his reflex against revealing that time travel and the Time Patrol existed. What remained was his duty.

Somehow he must get control of this horrible situation. Once he'd had a rest, let flesh and intelligence recover from the shocks they had suffered, he should have a pretty good chance of outwitting Castelar. No matter how quick on the uptake, the man would be overwhelmed by strangeness. At the moment, however, Tamberly was only half alive.

And Castelar sensed the weakness and hammered shrewdly, pitilessly on it.

"Tell me! No dawdling, no sly roundabouts. Out with the truth!" The sword slid partially from its scabbard and snicked back.

"The tale is long and hard, Don Luis—"

A boot caught Tamberly in the ribs. He rolled over and lay gasping. Pain went through him in waves. As if among thunders, he heard: 'Come, now. Speak."

He forced himself back to a sitting position, hunched beneath implacability. "Yes, I masqueraded as a friar, but with no unchristian intention," he coughed. "It was necessary. You see, there are evil men abroad who also have these engines. As it was, they sought to raid your treasure, and bore us two off—"

The interrogation went on. Had it been the Dominicans under whom Castelar studied, they who ran the Spanish Inquisition? Or had he simply learned how to deal with prisoners of war? At first Tamberly had a notion of concealing the time travel part. It slipped from him, or was jarred from him, and Castelar hounded it. Remarkable how swiftly he grasped the idea. None of the theory. Tamberly himself had just the ghostliest idea of that, which a science millennia beyond his people's was to create. The thought that space and time were united baffled Castelar, till he dismissed it with an oath and went on to practical questions. But he did come to realize that the machine could fly; could hover; could instantly be wherever and whenever else its pilot willed.

Perhaps his acceptance was natural. Educated men of the sixteenth century believed in miracles; it was Christian, Jewish, and Muslim dogma. They also lived in a world of revolutionary new discoveries, inventions, ideas. The Spanish, especially, were steeped in tales of chivalry and enchantment—would be, till Cervantes laughed that out of them. No scientist had told Castelar that travel into the past was physically impossible; no philosopher had listed the reasons why it was logically absurd. He met the simple fact.

Mutability, the danger of aborting an entire future, did seem to elude him. Or else he refused to let it curb him. "God will take care of the world," he stated, and went after knowledge of what he could do and how.

He readily imagined argosies faring between the ages, and it fired him. Not that he was much interested in the truly precious articles of that commerce: the origins of civilizations, the lost poems of Sappho, a performance by the greatest gamelan virtuoso who ever lived, three-dimensional pictures of art that would be melted down for a ransom . . . he thought of rubies and slaves and, foremost, weapons. It was reasonable to him that kings of the future would seek to regulate that traffic and bandits seek to plunder it.

"So you were a spy for your lord, and his enemies were surprised to find us when they came as thieves in the night, but by God's grace we are free again," he said. "What next?"

The sun was low. Thirst raged in Tamberly's throat. His head felt ready to break open, his bones to fall apart. Blurred in his vision, Castelar squatted before him, tireless and terrible.

"Why we . . . we should return . . . to my comrades in arms," Tamberly croaked. "They will reward you well and . . . bring you back to your proper place."

"Will they, now?" The grin was wolfish. "And what payment to me, at best? Nor am I sure you have spoken truth, Tanaquil. The single sure thing is that God has given this instrument into my hands, and I must use it for His glory and the honor of my nation."

Tamberly felt as if the words driven against him, hour after hour, had each been a fist. "What would you, then?"

Castelar stroked his beard. "I think first," he murmured, narrow-eyed, "yes, assuredly first, you shall teach me how to manage this steed." He bounced to his feet. "Up!"

He must well-nigh drag his prisoner to the timecycle.

I must lie, I must delay, at worst I must refuse and take my punishment. Tamberly couldn't. Exhaustion, pain, thirst, hunger betrayed him. He was physically incapable of resistance.

Castelar crouched over him, alert to every move, ready to pounce at the slightest suspicion; and Tamberly was too stupefied to deceive him.

Study the console between the steering bars. Press for the date. The machine recorded every shift it made through the continuum. Yes, they'd come far indeed into the past, the thirtieth century before Christ.

"Before Christ," Castelar breathed. "Why, of course, I can go to my Lord when he walked this earth and fall on my knees—"

At that instant of his ecstasy, a hale man might have given him a karate chop. Tamberly could merely sag across the saddles and reach for an activator. Castelar flung him aside like a sack a meal. He lay half conscious on the ground till the sword pricked him into creeping back up.

A map display. Location: near the coast of what would someday be southern Ecuador. At Castelar's behest, Tamberly made the whole world revolve on the screen. The Conquistador lingered a while over the Mediterranean. "Destroy the paynim," he murmured. "Regain the Holy Land."

With the help of the map unit, which could show a region at any scale desired, the space control was childishly simple to use. At least it was if a coarse positioning sufficed. Castelar agreed shrewdly that he'd better not try such a stunt as appearing inside a locked treasure vault before he'd had plenty of practice. Time settings were as easy, once he learned the post-Arabic numerals. He did that in minutes.

Facile operation was necessary. A traveler might have to get out of somewhere or somewhen in a hell of a rush. Flying, on the antigravity drive, paradoxically required more skill. Castelar made Tamberly show him those controls, then get on behind him for a test flight. "If I fall, you do too," he reminded.

Tamberly wished they would. At first they wobbled, he nearly lost his seat, but soon Castelar was gleefully in charge. He experimented with a time jump, went back half a day. Abruptly the sun was high, and on the magnifying scanner screen he saw himself and the other a mile below in the valley. That shook him. Hastily, he sprang toward sunset. With the space jump, he shifted close to the now deserted ground. After hovering for a minute, he made a bumpy landing.

They got off. "Ah, praise God!" Castelar cried. "His wonders and mercies are without end."

"Please," Tamberly begged, "could we go to the river? I'm nigh dead of thirst."

"Presently you may drink," Castelar answered. "Here is neither food nor fire. Let us find a better place."

"Where?" Tamberly groaned.

"I have thought upon this," Castelar said.

"Seeking your king, no, that would be to put myself in his power. He would reclaim this device that can mean so much to Christendom. Back to the night in Caxamalca? No, not at once. We could run afoul of the pirates, if not, then certainly my own great captain Pizarro. With due respect—it would be difficult. But if I come carrying invincible weapons, he will heed my counsel."

Amidst the inner murk bearing down on him, Tamberly remembered that the Indians of Perú were not fully subjugated when the Conquistadores fell into combat against each other.

"You tell me that you hail from some two thousand years after Our Lord," Castelar proceeded. "That age could be a good harbor for a while. You know your way about in it. At the same time, the marvels should not be too bewildering to me—if this invention was made long afterward, as you have said." Tamberly realized that he had no dream of automobiles, airplanes, skyscrapers, television. . . . He kept his tigerish wariness: "However, I would fain begin in a peaceful haven, a backwater where the surprises are few, and feel my way forward. Yes, if we can find one more person there, someone whose word I can compare with yours—" Explosively: "You heard. You must know. Speak!"

Light ran long and golden out of the west. Birds streamed home to roost in darkling trees. The river gleamed with water, water. Again Castelar used physical force. He was efficient about it.

Wanda . . . she'd be in the Galápagos in 1987, and God knew those islands were peaceful enough . . . Exposing her to this danger did worse than break the Patrol's directive; the kyradex had broken that within Tamberly, anyway. But she was as smart and resourceful, and almost as strong, as any man. She'd be loyal to her poor battered uncle. Her blonde beauty would distract Castelar, while he grew incautious of a mere female. Between them, the Americans could find or make an opportunity. . . .

Afterward, often and often, the Patrolman cursed himself. Yet it was not really himself that responded, by whimpers and jerks, to the urging of the warrior.

Maps and coordinates of the islands, which no man recorded in history would tread before 1535; some description of them; some explanation of what the girl did there (Castelar was amazed, until he remembered amazons in the medieval romances); something about her as a person; the likelihood that she would be surrounded by friends most of the time, but toward the end might well take occasion to hike off alone—Again it was the questions, the cunning carnivore mind, that hunted everything out into the open.

Dusk had fallen. Tropically rapid, it deepened toward night. Stars winked forth. A jaguar yowled.

"Ah, so." Castelar laughed, softly and joyously. "You have done well, Tanaquil. Not of your free will; nevertheless, you have earned surcease."

"Please, may I go drink?" Tamberly would have to crawl.

"As you wish. Abide here, though, so I can find you later. Otherwise I fear you will perish in this wilderness."

Dismay jagged through Tamberly. Roused, he sat straight in the grass, "What? We were leaving together!"

"No, no. I have scant trust in you yet, my friend. I will see what I can do for myself. Afterward—that is in the hands of God. Until I come fetch you, farewell."

Sky-glow sheened on helmet and corselet. The knight of Spain strode to the time machine. He mounted it. Luminous, the controls yielded to his fingers. "Sant'Iago and at them!" rang aloud. He lifted several yards into the air. There followed a puff, and he was gone.

12 MAY 2937 B. C.

Tamberly woke at sunrise. The riverside was wet beneath him. Reeds rustled in a low wind, water purled and clucked. Smells of growth filled his nostrils.

His entire body hurt. Hunger clawed at him. But his head was clear, healed of the kyradex confusion and the torments that had followed. He could think again, be a man again. He climbed stiffly to his feet and stood for a span inhaling coolness.

The sky reached pale blue, empty save for a flight of crows that cawed past and disappeared. Castelar had not returned. Maybe he'd allow extra time. Seeing himself from above had perturbed him. Maybe he wouldn't return. He could meet death, off in the future, or could decide he didn't give a damn about the false friar.

No telling. What I can do is try to nail down that he never does find me. I can try to stay free.

Tamberly began walking. He was weak, but if he husbanded his energy and followed the river, he should reach the sea. Chances were there'd be a settlement at the estuary. Humans had long since crossed over from Asia to America. They'd be primitive, but likely hospitable. With the skills he possessed, he could become important among them.

After that—already he had an idea.

22 JULY 1435

He lets go of me. I drop a few inches to the ground, lose my footing, fall. Bounce up again. Scramble back from him. Stop. Stare.

Still in the saddle, he smiles. Through the blood racketing in my ears, I hear: "Be not afraid, *señorita.* I beg your pardon for this rough treatment, but saw no other way. Now, alone, we can talk."

Alone! Look around. We're close to water, a bay, see those outlines against the sky, got to be Academy Bay near Darwin Station, only what became of the station? Of the road to Puerto Ayora? Matazarno bushes, Palo Santo trees, grass in clumps, cactus between, sparse. Empty, empty. Ashes of a campfire. Jesus Christ! The giant shell, gnawed bones of a tortoise! This man's killed a Galápagos tortoise!

"Please do not flee," he says. "I would simply have to overtake you. Believe me, your honor is safe. More safe than it would be anywhere else. For we are quite by ourselves in these islands, like Adam and Eve before the Fall."

Throat dry, tongue thick. "Who are you? What is this?"

He gets off his machine. Sweeps me a courtly bow. "Don Luis Ildefonso Castelar y Moreno, from Barracota in Castile, lately with the captain Francisco Pizarro in Perú, at your service, my lady."

He's crazy, or I am, or the whole world is. Again I wonder if I'm dreaming, hit my head, caught a fever, delirious. Sure doesn't feel that way.

Those are plants I know. They stay put. The sun's shifted overhead and the air's less warm, but the smells baked out of the earth, they're like always. A grasshopper chirrs. A blue heron flaps by. Could this be for *real*?

"Sit down," he says. "You are taken aback. Would you like a drink of water?" As if to soothe me: "I fetch it from elsewhere. This is a desolate country. But you are welcome to all you want."

I nod, do as he suggests. He picks a container off the ground, brings it in reach of me, steps off at once. Not to alarm the little girl. It's bucket, pink, cracked at the top, useable but scarcely worth keeping. He must have scrounged it from wherever it got tossed out. Even in those shacky little houses in the village, plastic's cheap.

Plastic.

Final touch. Practical joke. 'Tain't funny, God. Got to laugh anyway. Whoop. Howl.

"Be calm, *señorita*. I tell you, while you behave wisely you have nothing to fear. I will protect you."

That pig! I'm no ultrafeminist, but when a kidnapper starts patronizing me, too much. The laughter rattles down to silence. Rise. Brace muscles. They shiver a bit.

Somehow, regardless, I am no longer afraid. Coldly furious. At the same time, more aware than ever before. He stands in front of me as sharp as if a lightning flash lit him up. Not a big man; thin; but remember that strength of his. Hispanic features, all right, of the pure European kind, tanned practically black. Not in costume. Those clothes are faded, mended, grubby; vegetable dyes. Unwashed, like himself. Smell powerful but he doesn't really stink, it's an outdoor kind of odor. The ridged helmet, sweeping down to guard his neck, and the cuirass are tarnished. I see scratches in the steel. From battle? Sword hung at his left hip. Sheath at the right meant for a knife. It being gone, he must have butchered the tortoise and cut a skewer for roasting it with the sword. Firewood he could break off these parched branches. Yonder, a fire drill he made. Sinew for cord. He's been here a while.

Whisper. "Where is here?"

"Another island of the same archipelago. You know it as Santa Cruz. That is five hundred years hence. Today is one hundred years before the discovery."

Breathe slow and deep. Heart, take it easy. I've read my share of science fiction. Time travel. Only, a Spanish Conquistador!

"When are you from?"

"I told you. About a century in the future. I fared with the brothers Pizarro, and we overthrew the pagan king of Perú."

"No. I shouldn't understand you." Wrong, Wanda. I remember. Uncle Steve told me once. If I met a sixteenth-century Englishman, I'd have a devil of a time. Spelling didn't change (won't change) too much, but pronunciation did. Spanish is a more stable language.

Uncle Steve!

Cool it. Speak steadily. Can't quite. Look this man in the eyes, at least. "You mentioned my kinsman just before you . . . laid violent hands on me."

He sounds exasperated. "I did no more than was necessary. Yes, if you are indeed Wanda Tamberly, I know your father's brother." He peers like a cat at a mousehole. "The name he used among us was Esteban Tanaquil."

Uncle Steve a time traveler too? I can't help it, dizziness rushes through me.

I shake myself free of it. Don Luis Et Cetera sees I'm bewildered. Or else he knew I'd be. I think he wants to push things along, keep me off balance. Says, "I warned you he is in danger. That is true. He is my hostage, left in a wilderness where starvation will soon take him off, unless wild beasts do so first. It is for you to earn his ransom."

22 MAY 1987

Blink. We're there. Like a blow to the solar plexus. I almost fall off. Grab his waist. Face burrows into the roughness of his cloak.

Calm, lassie. He told you to expect this . . . transition. He's awed. Hasty in the wind, *"Ave-Maria-gratiae-plena—"* It's cold up here in heaven. No moon, but stars everywhere. Riding lights of a plane, blink, blink, blink.

The Peninsula tremendous, a sprawled galaxy, half a mile underneath us. White, yellow, red, green, blue, shining blood-flow of cars, from San Jose to San Francisco. Hulks of black to the left where the hills rise. Shimmering darkness to the right, the Bay, fire-streaked by the bridges. Towns glimpsed, clusters of sparks, on the far shore. About ten o'clock on a Friday evening.

How often have I seen this before? From airliners. A space-time bike hanging aloft, me in the buddy seat behind a man born almost five centuries ago, that's something else.

He masters himself. The sheer lion courage of him—except a lion wouldn't charge headlong into the unknown, the way those guys did after Columbus showed them half a world to plunder. "Is this the realm of Morgana la Hada?" he breathes.

"No, it's where I live, those are lamps you see, lamps in the streets and houses and . . . on the wagons. They move by themselves, the wagons, without horses. Yonder goes a flying vessel. But it can't skip from place to place and year to year like this one."

A superwoman wouldn't babble facts. She'd feed him a line, mislead him, use his ignorance to trap him somehow. Yeah, "somehow," that's the catch. I'm just me, and he's a superman, or pretty close to it. Natural selection, back in his day. If you weren't physically tough, you didn't live to have kids. And a peasant could be stupid, might even do better if he was, but not a military officer who didn't have a Pentagon to plan his moves for him. Also, those hours of questioning on Santa Cruz Island (which I, Wanda May Tamberly, am the first woman ever to walk on) have beaten me down. He never laid a hand on me, but he kept at it and kept at it. Eroded the resistance out of me. My main thought right now is that I'd better cooperate. Otherwise he could too easily make some blunder that'd kill us both and leave Uncle Steve stranded.

"I have thought the saints might dwell in such a blaze of glory," Luis murmurs. The cities he knew went black after dark. You needed a lantern to find your way. If it was a fine city, it put stepping stones down the middle of the sidewalkless streets, to keep you above the horse droppings and garbage.

He turns tactical. "Can we descend unseen?"

"If you're careful. Go slowly as I guide you." I recognize the Stanford campus, a mostly unlighted patch. Lean forward against him, left hand holding onto the cloak. These are well-designed seats; my knees will keep me in place. That's a mighty long drop, though. Reach right arm past his side. Point. "Toward there."

The machine tilts forward. We slant down. My nose fills with the scents of him. I've already noticed: pungent rather than sour, yes, very *macho*.

Got to admire him. A hero, on his own terms. Can't stop a sneaking wish that he'll get away with his desperate caper.

Whoa, girl. That's a pitfall. You've heard about kidnapped people, even tortured people, developing sympathy for their captors. Don't you be a Patty Hearst.

Still, damn it, what Luis has done is fantastic. Brains as well as bravery. Think back. Try, while we chase through the air, try to get straight in your mind what he told you, what you saw, what you figured out.

Hard to. He admitted a lot of confusion himself. Mainly he hews to his faith in the Trinity and warlike saints. He'll succeed, dedicating his victories to them, and become greater than the Holy Roman Emperor; or he'll die in the attempt and go to Paradise, all sins forgiven because what he did was in the cause of Christendom. Catholic Christendom.

Time travel for real. Some kind of *guarda del tiempo*, and Uncle Steve works for it. (Oh, Uncle Steve, while we laughed and chatted and went on family picnics and watched TV and played chess or tennis, this was behind your eyes.) Some kind of bandits or pirates also running loose through history, and isn't that a terrifying thought? Luis escaped from them, has this machine, has me for his wild purposes.

How he got at me—wrung the basic information out of Uncle Steve. I'm afraid to imagine how, though he claims he didn't do any permanent damage. Flitted to the Galápagos, established camp before the islands were discovered. Made cautious reconnaissance trips into the twentieth century, 1987 to be exact. He knew I'd be around then, and I was the one person he had any hope of . . . using.

The campsite's in the arboretum behind Darwin Station. He could safely leave the machine there for a few hours at a stretch, especially in the early morning or late afternoon and at night. Walk into town or around the area, minus his armor. Clothes look funny, but he's careful to approach only working-class locals, and they're used to crazy tourists. Wheedle some, browbeat some, maybe bribe some. I got the impression he stole money. Ruthless. Anyhow, a few shrewd inquiries, at well-spaced intervals. Found out things about this era. Found out things about me. Once he knew I'd gone off on terminal leave, and roughly where, he could hover too high for us to see, watch through that magnifying screen he showed me, wait for an opportunity, swoop. And here we are.

He *will* do these things, come September. This is Memorial Day weekend. He wanted me to bring him to my home at a time when nobody would disturb us. Mainly me. (What's it like, meeting yourself in the living flesh?) I'm with Dad and Mom and Suzy in San Francisco. Tomorrow we're bound for Yosemite. Won't be back till Monday evening.

He and I in my apartment. The other three units are vacant, I know, students also away for the holiday.

Well, I dare hope he'll continue "respecting my honor." He did make that nasty crack about me dressing like a man *o una puta*. Thank—well, be glad I had the wit to get up indignant and tell him this is respectable ladies' garb where I come from. He apologized, sort of. Said I was a white woman, in spite of being a heretic. Indian women's feelings didn't count, of course.

What will he do next? What does he want of me? I don't know. Probably he isn't sure either, yet. If I got the same chance he's got, how would I use it? It's a godlike power. Hard to stay sensible with those controls between your hands.

"Turn right. Slowly, now."

We've flown above University Avenue, across Middlefield, and yonder's the Plaza; my street's that-a-way. Yep. "Halt." We stop. I look past his shoulder at the square building, ten feet below us and twenty ahead. The windows glimmer blind.

"I have rooms in that upper story."

"Have you space for the chariot?"

Gulp. "Well, yes, in the largest chamber. A few feet—" how many, damn it?—"about three feet behind those panes at the very corner." I'm guessing the Spanish foot of his day is not too different from the English foot of mine.

Evidently not. He leans forward, peers, gauges. My pulse gallops. Sweat prickles my skin. He means to make a quantum jump through space (no, not really through space. Around it?) and appear in my living room. What if we come out in the middle of something?

Oh, he's experimented, in his Galápagos retreat. The nerve that that took! He's made discoveries. He tried to explain them to me. As near as I can follow it, put in twentieth century words, you pass directly from one set of space-time coordinates to another. Maybe it's through a "wormhole"—vague recollection of articles in *Scientific American, Science News, Analog*—and for a moment your dimensions equal zero, then as you expand into your destination volume, you displace whatever matter is there. Air molecules, obviously. Luis found out that if a small solid object is in the way, it gets pushed aside. A big object, and the machine, with you aboard, settles beside it, off the exact spot you punched for. Probably mutual displacement. Action equals reaction. Agreed, Sir Isaac?

There must be limits. Suppose he gets it badly wrong and we end up in the wall? Splintering studs, nails shoved through my guts, stucco and plaster like cannonballs, and a ten- or twelve-foot drop to the ground on this heavy thing.

"St. James be with us," he says. I feel his motions. Whoops!

We're here, inches above the floor. He sets us down. We're here.

Street glow dim through the windows. Get off.

Knees weak. Start. Stop—his grip on my arm like jaws. "Halt," he commands.

"I only want to give us better light."

"I will make quite sure of that, my lady." He comes along. When I flick the switch and everything turns bright, he gasps. His fingers close bruisingly hard. "Ow!" He lets go and stares around him.

Must have seen electric bulbs on Santa Cruz. 111 But Puerto Ayora's a poor little village, and I don't suppose he peeped into the station personnel's quarters. Try to look at this through his eyes. Difficult. I take it all for granted. How much can he actually *see*, as alien as it is to him?

Bike fills most of the rug. Crowds my desk, the sofa, the entertainment cabinet and bookshelf. I knocked two chairs over. Fourth wall, door open on the short hall. Bathroom and broom closet to the left, bedroom and clothes closet to the right, kitchen at the end, those doors closed. Cubbyholes. And I'll bet nobody less than a merchant prince lived like this in the sixteenth century.

What immediately astounds him: "So many books? You cannot be a cleric."

Why, I doubt if I have a hundred, texts included. And Gutenberg was before Columbus, wasn't he?

"How poorly bound they are." That seems to renew his confidence. I suppose books were still scarce and expensive. And no paperbacks.

He shakes his head at a couple of magazines;

the covers must seem downright garish. Harshness again. "You will show me these lodgings."

I do, explaining things as best I can. He has glimpsed (will glimpse) faucets and flush toilets in Puerto Ayora. "How I wish for a bath," I sigh. Give me a hot shower and clean clothes, you can keep your Paradise, Don Luis.

"Presently, if you like. However, it shall be in my sight, like all else you do."

"What? Even the, uh, even that?"

He's embarrassed but determined. "I regret this, my lady, and will keep my face averted, save that I must see enough to be certain you make ready no trick. For I believe yours to be a valiant soul, and you have mysteries and devices that I do not fathom at your beck."

Ha. If only I did keep a .45 under my lingerie. At that, I've a bit of trouble convincing him the upright vacuum cleaner isn't a gun. He makes me lug it into the living room and demonstrate. A grin turns him human. "Give me a charwoman," he says. "She doesn't howl like a mad wolf."

We leave it where it is and return down the hall. In the kitchen-dinette, he admires the pilot-lighted gas range. Tell him, "I need a sandwich—food—and a beer. What about you? Tepid water and half-cooked tortoise for days."

"Do you offer me hospitality?" He sounds amazed.

"Call it that."

He ponders. "No, my thanks, but I cannot in conscience eat your salt."

Funny how touching that is. "Old-fashioned, aren't you? If I remember rightly, the Borgias were in business in your time. Or was that earlier? Well, let us agree we're opponents who've sat down to negotiate."

He inclines his head, takes off his helmet and sets it on the counter. "My lady is most gracious."

A snack will do me a lot of good. And maybe disarm him. I am an attractive wench when I choose to be. Learn as much as possible. Keep alert. And beneath the tension—damn it, this is flat-out fascinating.

He watches me start the coffeemaker. He's interested when I open the fridge, startled when I pop the tops on a couple of brews. I take a sip from the first and hand it to him. "Not poisoned, you see. Take a chair." He settles himself at the table. I get busy with bread and cheese and stuff.

"A curious drink," he says. Surely they had beer in his time, but doubtless it was quite different from ours.

"I have wine, if you'd rather."

"No, I must not dull my senses."

Beer in California wouldn't get a cat tiddly. Too bad.

"Tell me more about yourself, Lady Wanda."

"If you'll do likewise for me, Don Luis."

I serve us. We talk. What a life he's led! He

finds mine just as remarkable. Well, I am a woman. By his lights, I should have devoted my efforts to breeding, housekeeping, and prayers. Unless I was Queen Isabella—Rein it in. Make him underestimate you.

That requires technique. I'm not used to flapping my lashes and cheering a man on to describe how wonderful he is. Can do it when called for, though. One way to keep a date from deteriorating into a wrestling match. Never date that kind twice. Give me a guy who considers himself my equal.

Luis isn't the swinish sort either. He's keeping his promise, absolutely polite. Unyielding, but polite. A killer, a racist, a fanatic; a man of his word, fearless, ready to die for king or comrade; Charlemagne dreams, tender little memories of his mother, poor and proud in Spain. Kind of humorless, but a flaming romantic.

Glance at my watch. Close to midnight. Good Lord, have we sat here that long?

"What do you mean to do, Don Luis?"

"Obtain weapons of your country."

Level voice. Smile on lips. Sees my shock. "Are you surprised, my lady? What else could I seek? I would not abide in this place. From above, it may resemble the gates of Heaven, but I think down on earth, those engines rushing and roaring demonic in their thousands must make it more akin to Hell. Foreign folk, foreign language, foreign ways. Heresy and shamelessness rampant, no? Forgive me. I believe you are chaste, in spite of those garments. But are you not an infidel? Clearly, you defy God's law concerning the proper status of women." He shakes his head. "No, I will return to that age which is mine and my country's. Return well armed."

Appalled: "How?"

He tugs his beard. "I have given thought to this. A Wagon of your kind would be of small use or none where there are neither roads nor fuel for it. Moreover, it would at best be a clumsy steed, set beside my gallant Florio—or the chariot I have captured. However, you must have firearms as far beyond our muskets and cannon as those are beyond the spears and bows of the Indios. Hand-held, yes, that would be best."

"But, but I haven't any weapons. I can't get any."

"You know what they are like and where they are kept. In military arsenals, for example. I will have much to ask you in the days to come. Thereafter, why, I have the means to pass unseen by bolts and bars, and carry off what I wish."

True. Chances are he'll succceed. He'll have me, first for briefing, later for guide. No way do I get out of that, unless I'm heroic and make him kill me. Which would leave him free to try elsewhere, and Uncle Steve forsaken wherever-whenever he is.

"How—how will you—use those guns?"

Solemn: "In the end, marshal the armies of the Emperor and lead them to victory. Hurl back the

Turks. Uproot the Lutheran sedition in the North that I've heard of. Humble the French and English. The final Crusade." Draws breath. "First, I should assure the conquest of the New World and my own power within it. Not that I am more greedy for fame than others. But God has appointed me to this."

My mind spins through the insanity of what would follow from the least of his projects. "But everything around us now, it'll never have been! I'll never have been born!"

He crosses himself. "That is as God wills. However, if you give faithful service, I can take you back with me and see to your well-being."

Yeah. Well-being á la sixteeth-century Spanish female. If I exist. My parents wouldn't have, would they? I've no idea. I'm simply convinced Luis is juggling forces beyond his imagining, or mine, or anybody's except maybe that Time Guard—like a child playing on a snowfield ripe for an avalanche—

The Time Guard! That Everard man last year. Asking about Uncle Steve, why? Because Stephen Tamberly didn't really work for a scientific foundation. He worked for the Time Guard.

Their job has got to include heading off disasters. Everard gave me his card. Phone number on it. Where'd I put that bit of cardboard? Tonight the universe is balanced on it.

"I should begin by learning what did happen in Perú after I . . . left it," Luis is saying. "Then I can plan how to amend the tale. Tell me."

Shudder. Shake off the sense of nightmare. Think what to *do*. "I can't. How should I know? It was more than four hundred years ago." Solid, sinewy, sweaty, a ghost from that vanished past sits across from me, behind soiled plates, coffee cups, and beer cans.

Eruption in my head.

Hold voice low. Look downward. Demure. "We have history books, of course. And libraries that everyone may enter. I'll go find out."

He chuckles. "You are bold, my lady. However, you shall not leave these rooms, nor be out of my sight, until I am certain of my mastery of things. When I venture forth—to look about, or sleep, or for whatever reason—I will return to the same minute as I departed. Avoid the middle of the floor."

Time machine appears in the same space as me. Boom! No, likelier it'd be jarred aside a few inches. I'd be thrown against the wall. Could break bones, uselessly.

"Well, I c-can talk to somebody who knows the history. We have . . . devices . . . for sending speech through wires, across miles. There's one in the main room."

"And how shall I tell whom you speak with or what you say in your English tongue? Most assuredly, you shall lay no hand on that engine." He doesn't know what a phone looks like, but I couldn't begin to use mine before he realized.

The hostility drops. Earnest: "My lady, I pray

you, understand that I bear no ill will. I do what I must. Those are my friends yonder, my country, my Church. Have the wisdom—the compassion—to accept that? I know you are learned. Do you have any book of your own that may help? Remember, whatever happens, I am going ahead with my sacred mission. You can make the course of it less terrible for those who you love."

Excitement ebbs away with hope. I feel how tired I am. An ache in every cell of me. Cooperate in this. Maybe afterward he'll let me sleep. What dreams may come couldn't possibly be as bad as my wakefulness.

The encyclopedia. Birthday present from Suzy a couple of years ago, my sister, who's doomed if Spain will have conquered Europe, the Near East, and both the Americas.

Ice-thrill. I remember! I dropped Everard's card in a desk drawer, upper left, where I keep miscellany. Phone right above, beside the typewriter.

"Señorita, you tremble."

"Haven't I reason to?" Rise. "Come." The cold wind through me whistles the exhaustion out. "I do have a book or two that may have information."

He follows directly behind. His presence is a shadow over me, a shadow with weight.

At the desk, "Hold! What do you want from that drawer?"

I never was a good liar. Can keep my face turned away, and a wobble in my voice is to be expected. "You see how many the volumes are. I must consult my record of them, to locate the chronicle. Watch. No hidden arquebus." Whip it open before he grabs my wrist. Stand passive, let him paw through, satisfy himself. The card skips amongst the clutter. Like my pulse.

"I beg your pardon, my lady. Give me no occasion to suspect you, and I will give you no roughness."

Flip the card right side up. Make that look accidental. Read again: Manson Everard, midtown Manhattan address, the phone number, the phone number. Cram that into my mind. Scratch about. What can I palm off as a sort of library catalogue? Ah, my auto insurance policy. Had it out for a look after that fender-bender months ago—no, last month, April—and haven't—hadn't—gotten around to putting it back in the safe deposit. Make a show of studying it. "Ah, here we are."

Okay, now I know how to call for help. Opportunity to do it is lacking. Stay watchful.

Sidle past the time bike to the bookshelf. Luis treads close against me. *Payn to Polka*. Take it out, page through. He looks across my shoulder. Exclaims when he recognizes *Peru*. He's literate. Not in English, though.

Translate. Early history. Pizarro's journey to Túmbez, the awful hardships, his eventual return to Spain in search of backing. "Yes, yes, I have heard, how often I have heard." To Panamá in 1530, Túm-

bez in 1531, "I was with him." Fighting. A small
detachment makes an epic trek over the mountains.
Entry into Cajamarca, capture of the Inca, his ransom. "And then, and then?" Judicial murder of
Atahuallpa. "Oh, bad. Well, no doubt my captain
decided it was necessary." March to Cuzco. Almagro's expedition to Chile. Pizarro founds Lima.

Manco, his puppet Inca, escapes, raises the people
against the invaders. Cuzco besieged from early
February 1536 till Almagro comes back and relieves
it in April 1537; meanwhile, desperate valor on both
sides, throughout the country. Right after the hard-
won Spanish victory, Indians still waging guerrilla
warfare, the Pizarro brothers and Almagro fall out
with each other. Pitched battle in 1538, Almagro
defeated and executed. His half-caste son and
friends embittered; conspire; assassinate Francisco
Pizarro in Lima, 26 June 1541. "No! Body of Christ,
this shall not happen!" Charles V has sent a new
governor, who now takes over, beats the Almagro
faction, and beheads the young man. "Horrible,
horrible. Christian against Christian. No, it is clear,
we require a strong man to take leadership at the
earliest moment of misfortune."

Luis draws his sword. What the hell? Alarmed,
I drop the volume, back off past the machine toward
my desk. He falls on his knees. Lifts the sword by
the blade, makes it a cross. Tears run down the
leather cheeks, into the midnight beard. "Almighty
God, holy Mother of God," he sobs, "be with Your
servant."

A chance? No time to think.

Grab the upright vacuum cleaner. Swing it on high. He hears, turns on his knees, crouches to bound up. A heavy awkward club. Give it everything my arms and shoulders have got. Across the bike, crash the motor end onto his bare head.

He sags. Blood flows like crazy, neon-light red. Lacerated scalp. Have I knocked him out? Don't stop to check. Let the vac clatter down on top of him. Leap to the phone.

Buzz-zz. The number? I'd better have it right. Punch-punch-punch— Luis groans. He hauls himself to all fours. Punch-punch.

Ring.

Ring. Ring. Luis takes hold of a shelf, clambers his way to a stance.

The remembered voice. "Hello. This is Manse Everard's answering machine."

Oh, God, no!

Luis shakes his head, wipes the blood from his eyes. His head is smeared, it drips, impossibly much, impossibly brilliant.

"I'm sorry I can't come to the phone. If you wish to leave a message, I'll get back to you soon's may be."

Luis stands slumped, his arms dangle, but he glares at me. "So," he mumbles. "Treachery."

"You may begin talking when you hear the beep. Thank you."

He stoops, takes up his sword, advances. Unevenly, inexorably.

Scream, "Wanda Tamberly. Palo Alto. Time traveler." What's the date, what the hell's the date? "Friday night before Memorial Day. Help!"

The sword point is at my throat. "Drop that thing," he snarls. I do. He's got me backed against the desk. "I should kill you for this. Perhaps I will."

Or forget his scruples about my virtue and—

And at least I left a clue for Everard. Didn't I?

Whoosh. The second machine above the first, its riders flattening themselves below the ceiling.

Luis yells. Scuttles backward, onto the driver's saddle of his. Sword in hand. Other hand dances on the controls. Everard's hampered. I see a gun in his fist. But whoosh. Luis is gone.

Everard sets down.

Whirling, keening, darkening. I never passed out before. If I can just sit for a minute.

23 MAY 1987

She came in from the hallway wearing a bathrobe over her pajamas. Its snugness brought forth a lithe figure, its blueness the hue of her eyes. Sunlight through the west window made gold of her hair.

She blinked. "Oh, my. Afternoon," she murmured. "How long have I slept?"

Everard had risen from the sofa where he'd sat with one of her books. "About fourteen hours, I guess," he said. "You needed it. Welcome back."

She stared around. There was no timecycle, nor any bloodstains. "After my partner tucked you in bed, she and I fetched supplies and cleaned up the mess as best we could," Everard explained. "She took off. No point in cluttering your place. A guard was necessary, of course, as a precaution. Better check around at your convenience and make sure everything is in order. Wouldn't do for your earlier self to return and find traces of the ruckus. You didn't, after all."

Wanda sighed. "No, never a hint."

"We've got to prevent paradoxes like that. The situation is tangled enough as is." *And dangerous,* Everard thought. *More than deadly dangerous. I should hearten her.* "Hey, I'll bet you're starved."

He liked the way she laughed. "Could eat the proverbial horse with a side of French fries, and apple pie for dessert."

"Well, I took the liberty of laying in some groceries, and could use lunch myself, if you don't mind my joining you."

"Mind? Try not to!"

In the kitchen he urged that she be seated while he put the meal together. "I'm a pretty competent man with a steak and a salad. You've been through the meat grinder. Most people would be in a daze."

"Thanks." She accepted. For a minute, only the sounds of him at work broke the silence. Then, her look steady upon him, she said, "You belong to the Time Guard, don't you?"

"Huh?" He glanced about. "Yes. In English, it's usually the Time Patrol." He paused. "Outsiders aren't supposed to know that time travel goes on. We can't tell them unless authorized, and that's just when circumstances warrant. Clearly they do in this case; you've crashed into the fact. And I have authority to make the decision. I'll level with you, Miss Tamberly."

"Great. How did you find me? When I got your answering machine, I was in despair."

"You're new to the concept. Think. After I'd played your message, what'd you expect me to do but mount an expedition? We hovered outside the window, saw that man threatening you, hopped inside. Unfortunately, I was too crowded to get a shot at him before he vamoosed."

"Why didn't you jump back in time?"

"And save you some unpleasant hours? Sorry. I'll tell you later about the hazards of changing the past."

She frowned. "I know a bit already."

"Hm, I suppose you do. Look, we needn't discuss this till you feel recovered. Take a couple of days and get over the shock."

She lifted her head pridefully. "Thanks, but no need. I'm unhurt, hungry, and eaten alive by curiosity. Concern, too. My uncle—No, really, please, I'd much rather not wait."

"Wow, you're a tough cookie. Okay. Let's start by you telling me your experiences. Take it slow. I'll interrupt you a lot with questions. The Patrol needs to know everything. Needs it more than you're aware."

"And the world is?" She shivered, swallowed, clenched fingers on the tabletop edge, launched into her story. They were halfway through their meal before he had exhausted it of detail.

Starkly, he said, "Yes, this is very bad. Be a lot worse if you hadn't proved so courageous and resourceful, Miss Tamberly."

She flushed. "Please, I'm Wanda."

He forced a smile. "All right, I'm Manse. Spent my boyhood in Middle America of the 1920s and '30s. The manners they installed have stuck. But if you prefer first names, that's fine by me."

She gave him a long look. "Yes, you would stay a polite country boy, wouldn't you? Roving through history, you'd miss out on the social changes in your homeland."

Intelligent, he thought. *And beautiful, in a strong-boned fashion.*

Anxiety touched her. "What about my uncle?"

He winced. "I'm sorry. The Don told you nothing more than that he left Steve Tamberly on the same continent but in the far past. No location, no date."

"You have—time to search for him."

He shook his head. "I wish we did, but we don't. We could use up thousands of man-years. And we haven't got them. The Patrol's stretched too thin. We're barely enough to carry out our normal missions and try to cope with emergencies like this. Only so many man-years available, you see, because sooner or later every agent is bound to die or be disabled. Here events have gotten out of hand. We'll need every resource we can spare to set matters right—if we can."

"Might Luis go back for him?"

"Maybe. I suspect not. He'll have more important things in mind. Hide out till his injury heals, and then—" Everard stared past her. "A hard, smart, unmerciful, reckless man, loose on a machine. He could appear anywhere, anywhen. The harm he can do is unlimited."

"Uncle Steve—"

"He might be able to help himself. I'm not sure how, but he may hit on a plan, if he survives. He's bright and strong. I see now why you've been his favorite relative."

She dabbed at a tear. "Damn it, I will not bawl!

Maybe later—maybe later we'll find a clue. Meanwhile, m-my steak's getting cold." She attacked it as if it were an enemy.

He resumed his own eating. In an odd way, the silence between them changed from strained to companionable. After a while she asked quietly, "How about telling me the whole truth?"

"An outline of it," he agreed. "That alone will take a couple of hours."

131

—In the end she sat wide-eyed on the sofa while he paced before her, to and fro. His fist hammered his palm. "A Ragnarok situation," he said. "But not hopeless. Wanda, whatever has become or will become of Stephen Tamberly, he did not live in vain. Through Castelar, he passed two words on to you, *Exaltationists* and *Vilcabamba*. Not that I imagine Castelar would have done it if you hadn't had the wits—under those conditions, at that—to lead him on, get him to tell what he knew."

"That was very little," she demurred.

"A bomb can be small too, till it explodes. Look, the Exaltationists—I'll tell you more in due course, but briefly, they're a gang of desperados from the rather far future. Outlaws in their milieu; snatched several vehicles and escaped into space-time tracklessness. We've had to cope with results of their doings before now—'before now' in terms of my life, that is—but they've always avoided capture. Well, you've told me they were in Vilcabamba. Archaeologists these days disagree about its identity, but ours have learned that Bingham was right and it was in fact Machu Picchu. From the descriptions you got out of Castelar, the date must be soon after the last native resistance to the Spaniards was crushed. That's a sufficient lead for our scouts to locate the scene exactly.

132

"An agent of ours had 'already' reported outsiders active in the court of the Inca, some years before Pizarro arrived. It seems they tried and failed to head off a division of the royal power, which led to civil war and paved the way for that corporal's guard of invaders. In the light of what you've told me, I'm sure they were the Exaltationists, attempting to change history. When it didn't work, they decided they'd at least hijack Atahuallpa's ransom. That'd be disruptive enough, and could well enable them to do still more mischief."

"Why?" she whispered.

"Why, to abort the whole future. Make themselves overlords, first in America, eventually throughout the world. There'd never have been a you or a me, a United States, a Danellian destiny, a Time Patrol . . . unless they organized one of their own to protect the misshapen history they brought into being. Not that I think they could long have stayed in charge. Selfishness like that generally turns on itself. Battles through time, a chaos of changes—I wonder how much flux the space-time fabric could survive."

She whitened, then whistled. ''Ye gods, Manse!''

He stopped his prowling, leaned over, touched her below the chin to bring her face upward toward his, and asked with a crooked smile, "How does it feel knowing you may have saved the universe?"

15 APRIL 1610

The spacecraft was black, lest they on Earth see a star pass over them, swift before sunrise or after sunset, and know they were watched. Nevertheless, a broad one-way transparency filled it with light. It was orbiting dayside when Everard arrived, and the planet stretched vast, blue swirled with white around the ruddinesses that were continents.

His cycle appeared in the receiver bay and he jumped off without pausing to love the sight as he had done often and often. The gravitor put full weight under his feet. He hastened to the pilot deck. Three agents whom he knew, though centuries sundered their births, awaited him.

"We believe we've acquired the moment," said Umfanduma immediately. "Here's the playback."

Another vessel, of those that between them kept Machu Picchu under surveillance, had taken the data. This was the command ship. Everard had come as soon as messages transmitted through space relayed through time reached him. The image was from minutes earlier. At ultramagnification after light had crossed atmosphere, it was blurry. Yet when Everard froze its motion and peered closer, he saw metal shine on the head and torso of a man. That one and another were getting to their feet beside a timecycle, on a platform where the view swept from end to end of the great dead city, on to the mountains around. Dark-clad people crowded near.

He nodded. "Got to be," he said. "We don't

know just when Castelar will make his break for freedom, but I'd guess it as within the next two or three hours. What we want to do is hit the Exaltationists right afterward."

Not before, because that did not happen. We dare not undermine even this forbidden pattern of events. The enemy dares do anything. That is why we must destroy him.

138

Umfanduma frowned. "Tricky," she said. "They always keep a machine aloft, well equipped with detectors. I'm sure they're prepared to flee at an instant's notice."

"Uh-huh. However, their scooters are too few to carry them all at once. They'd have to ferry. Or else, likelier, abandon those who aren't so lucky as to be right by the transportation. We won't need many of our own. Let's get organized."

In the span that followed, the ships filled with armed vehicles and their riders. Tight-beamed communications flickered back and forth. Everard developed his plan, gave out his assignments.

Thereafter he must stand by, try to keep his nerves quiet, abide the word. He found it helpful to think about Wanda Tamberly.

"Now!"

He leaped to the saddle. Gunner Tetsuo Motonobu was already in place. Everard's fingers flew over the console.

They hung aloft in enormous azure. A condor wheeled afar. The mountainscape spread beneath, a majestic labyrinth, intensely green save where snow flashed on peaks or gorges plunged in shadows. Machu Picchu was mightiness in stone. What would the civilization that created it have done, had fate allowed it to live?

Again Everard could not pause to wonder. The Exaltationist sentry hovered yards off. He saw the man clearly in thin air and candent sunlight, astounded but fierce, snatching for a sidearm. Motonobu fired his energy gun. Lightning flared, thunder crashed. The man dropped charred from his mount and fell as Lucifer fell. Smoke trailed him. The vehicle wavered out of control.

We'll take care of it later. Down!

Everard didn't overjump the space between. He wanted an overview. As he power-dived, wind roared around an invisible force screen. The buildings swelled in his vision.

His fellow Patrolmen were raking them with fire. Bolts flew hell-colored. When Everard got there, the battle was over.

—Evening yellowed the western sky. Night rose from the valleys to lap ever higher around the walls of Machu Picchu. It had grown chilly and hushed.

Everard left the house he had used for interrogation. Two agents stood outside. "Round up the rest of the squad, bring out the prisoners, prepare to return to base," he said wearily.

"Have you learned something, sir?" asked Motonobu.

Everard shrugged. "Something. The intelligence staff will get more out of them, of course, though I doubt it'll prove of much use. I did find one who's willing to cooperate in return for a promise of comfortable surroundings on the exile planet. Trouble is, he doesn't know what I wish he did."

"Where-when those that got away have gone?"

Everard nodded. "The ringleader, name of Merau Varagan, took a bad sword wound when Castelar fought free. A couple of his men were about to whisk him off to a distination he alone knew to tell them, for medical care. So they were in position to scram with him when we showed up. Three more managed it too."

He straightened. "Ah," he said, "we succeeded as well as could be looked for. The bulk of the gang are dead or under arrest. The few who escaped must have scattered randomly. They may never find each other. The conspiracy's broken."

Motonobu's tone was wistful. "If only we could have come earlier, arranged a proper trap. We'd have bagged the lot."

"We couldn't because we didn't," said Everard sharply. "We are the law, remember?"

"Yes, sir. What I also remember is that crazy Spaniard and the havoc he may yet make. How're we going to track him down . . . before it's too late?"

Everard made no reply, but turned toward the esplanade where the vehicles were parked. To the east he saw the Gate of the Sun on its ridge, etched black against heaven.

24 MAY 1987

Wanda let him in when he knocked on her door. "Hi!" she exclaimed breathlessly. "How are you? How'd things go?"

"They went," he said.

She took both his hands. Her voice softened. "I've been so worried about you, Manse."

That felt almighty good to hear. "Oh, I take care of my hide. The operation, well, we nabbed most of the bandits without loss to ourselves. Machu Picchu is clean once more." *Was clean. Was left in its loneliness for another three centuries. Now tourists halloo everywhere. But a Patrolman shouldn't pass judgments. He needs to be case-hardened if he's to work in the history of humankind.*

"Marvelous!" Impulsively, she hugged him. He hugged back. They retreated in a slight, shared confusion.

"If you'd come ten minutes ago, you wouldn't've found me," she said. "I couldn't sit and do nothing. Went for a long, long walk."

Dismayed, he snapped, "I told you not to leave this place! You aren't safe. We've planted an instrument here that'll warn of any intruder, but we can't trail around after you. Damnation, girl, Castelar's still at large."

She wrinkled her nose at him. "Better I should climb these walls? Why would he chase after me again?"

"You were his single twentieth-century contact. You could possibly give us a lead to him. Or so he may fear."

She grew serious. "As a matter of fact, I can."

"Huh? What do you mean?"

She tugged his hand. How warm hers was. "C'mon, relax, let me fetch us a beer, and we'll talk. That hike I took cleared my head. I started thinking back, reliving the whole business, except free of terror and unfamiliarity. And, yes, I believe I can tell you what point Luis is bound to make for."

He stood where he was. His pulse slugged. "How?"

The blue eyes searched him. "I did get to know the man," she said low. "Not what you'd call intimately, but the relationship sure was intense while it lasted. He isn't a monster. By our standards he's cruel, but he's a son of his era. Ambitious and greedy—and in his heart a knight-errant. I searched my memory, minute by minute. Kind of stood outside and watched the two of us. And I saw how he reacted when he learned the Indians would rebel and besiege Francisco Pizarro's brothers in Cuzco, and the troubles that would follow. If he appears as if by miracle and raises the siege, that'll put him straightaway in command of the whole shebang. But over and above any such calculations, Manse, he has got to be there. His honor calls him."

6 FEBRUARY 1536

(JULIAN CALENDAR)

In the upland dawn, the imperial city burned. Fire arrows and rocks wrapped in blazing oil-soaked cotton flew like meteors. Thatch and wood kindled. Stone walls enclosed furnaces. Flames howled high, sparks showered, smoke roiled thick on the wind. Soot dulled the rivers where they met. Through the noise, conchs lowed, throats shrieked. In their tens of thousands, the Indios seethed around Cuzco. They were a brown tide, out of which tossed chieftainly banners, feather crests, copper-edged axes and spears. They surged against the thin Spanish lines, smote, struggled, recoiled in blood and turmoil, billowed again forward.

Castelar arrived above a citadel that brooded north of the combat. He glimpsed its massiveness filled with natives. For an instant he wanted to swoop down, kill and kill and kill. But no, yonder was where his comrades fought. Sword in right hand, left on the helm board, he rushed through the air to their deliverance.

What matter if he had failed to bring guns from the future? His blade was sharp, his arm strong, and the archangel of war winged over his bare head. Nonetheless he kept wholly alert. Foes might lurk in this sky or snap forth out of nowhere. Let him be ready to jump through time, evade pursuit, return to strike swiftly again and again, as a wolf slashes at an elk.

He swept above a central square, where a great building raged with conflagration. Horsemen trotted down a street. Their steel flashed, their pennons streamed. They were bound on a sally, out into the enemy horde.

Castelar's decision sprang into being. He would veer off, wait a few minutes, let them become engaged, and then smite. With such an avenging eagle on their side, the Spanish would know God had heard him, and hew a road through foemen smitten with panic.

Some saw him pass over. He glimpsed upturned faces, heard cries. There followed a thunder of gallop, a deep-toned "Sant'Iago and at them!"

He crossed the southern bounds of the city, banked, swung about for his onslaught. Now that he knew this machine, how splendidly it responded to him — his horse of the wind, that he would ride into liberated Jerusalem — and at last, at last, into the presence of the Savior on earth?

Ya-a-a!

Alongside him, another flyer, two men upon it. His fingers stabbed for the controls. Agony seared. "Mother of God, have mercy!" His steed was slain. It toppled through emptiness. At least he would die in battle. Though the forces of Satan had prevailed against him, they would not against the gates of Heaven that stood wide for Christ's soldier.

His soul whirled from him, away into night.

24 MAY 1987

"The ambush worked almost perfectly," Carlos Navarro reported to Everard. "When we spotted him from space, we activated the electromagnetic generator and jumped to his vicinity. The field it projected induced voltages that caused his machine to give him a severe electric shock. Disabled it, too, scrambled the electronics. But you know this. We gave him a stun shot to make sure and plucked him out of the air before he hit the ground. Meanwhile the cargo carrier appeared, scooped up the crippled vehicle, and made off. Everything was complete in less than two minutes. I suppose a number of men glimpsed us, but it would have been fleetingly, and in the general confusion of battle."

"Good work," said Everard. He leaned back in his shabby old armchair. His New York apartment surrounded them, comfortable with souvenirs—Bronze Age helmet and spears above the bar, polar bear rug from Viking Age Greenland on the floor, stuff such as would not cause outsiders to wonder much but did hold memories for him.

He hadn't gone on the mission. No reason thus to waste an Unattached agent's lifespan. There had been no danger, except that Castelar would be too quick and get away. The electric gimmick prevented that.

"As a matter of fact," he said, "your operation is part of history." He gestured at the volume of Prescott on an end table beside him. "I've been reading that. The Spanish chronicles describe appa-

ritions of the Virgin above the burning hall of Vira-
cocha, where the cathedral was later built, and of
St. James on the battlefield, inspiring the troops.
That's generally taken to be a pious legend, or an
account of hysterical illusions, but— Ah, well.
How's the prisoner?"

"When I left him, he was resting under seda-
tion," Navarro replied. "His burns will heal without
scars. What will they do with him?"

"That depends on a number of things." Everard
took his pipe from the ashtray where he had laid it
and coaxed it back to life. "High on the list is
Stephen Tamberly. You know about him?"

"Yes." Navarro scowled. "Unfortunately,
though unavoidably, the current surge through the
vehicle wiped the molecular record of where and
when it's traveled. Castelar's gotten a preliminary
kyradex quiz—we knew you'd want to know—and
doesn't recall the place and date he left Tamberly at,
merely that it was thousands of years ago and near
the Pacific coast of South America. He knew he
could retrieve the exact data if he wanted to, and
rather doubted he would. Therefore he didn't bother
memorizing the coordinates."

Everard sighed. "I was afraid of that. Poor
Wanda."

"Sir?"

"Never mind." Everard consoled himself with
smoke. "You may leave. Go out on the town and
enjoy yourself."

"Wouldn't you like to come along?" Navarro asked diffidently.

Everard shook his head. "I'll sit tight for a while. It's barely possible that Tamberly found some way to get rescued. If so, he was brought first to one of our bases for debriefing, and inquiry has shown I'm involved in his case, and I'll be informed. Naturally, that couldn't be before we wind up this job otherwise. Maybe I'll get a call soon."

153

"I see. Thank you. Goodbye."

Navarro departed. Everard settled back down. Dusk seeped into the room, but he didn't turn on the lights. He wanted just to sit thinking, and quietly hoping.

18 AUGUST 2930 B.C.

Where the river met the sea, the village clus-
tered its houses of clay. Only two dugout canoes lay
drawn up on the shore, for fishers were out on this
calm day. Most women were likewise gone, cultivat-
ing small patches of gourd, squash, potato, and
cotton at the edge of the mangrove swamp. Smoke
lifted slow from the communal fire that an old
person always tended. Other women and aged men
had tasks to do in their homes, while small children
took care of smaller. Folk wore brief skirts of twisted
fiber, ornaments of shell, teeth, feathers. They
laughed and chattered.

The Vesselmaker sat cross-legged in the doorway of his dwelling. Today he did not shape pots
and bowls or bake them hard. Instead, he stared
into space and kept silence. He often did since he
learned the speech of men and began his wondrous
labors. It must be respected. He was kindly, but
these fits came upon him. Perhaps he planned a
beautiful new piece of work, or perhaps he com-
muned with spirits. Certainly he was a special being, with his great height, pale skin and hair and
eyes, enormous whiskers. A cape decked him
against the sun, which he found harsher than common folk did. Inside the house, his woman ground
wild seed in her mortar. Their two living infants
slept.

Shouts arose. The field tillers swarmed into
sight. People in the village hurried to see what this
meant. The Vesselmaker rose and followed them.

Along the riverbank came a stranger striding. Visitors were frequent, mainly bringing trade goods, but nobody had seen this man before. He looked much like anyone else, though heavier-muscled. His garb was noticeably different. Something hard and shiny rested in a sheath on his hip.

Where could he be from? Surely hunters would days ago have noticed a newcomer making his way down the valley. The women squealed when he hailed them. The old men gestured them back and offered seemly greeting.

The Vesselmaker arrived.

For a long while Tamberly and the explorer stood gaze upon gaze. *He's of the local race.* Odd how calm the knowledge was in him, now when at last time had brought him to the goal of his yearnings. *Would be. Best not to raise extra questions, even in the heads of simple Stone Agers. How'd he plan to explain that sidearm?*

The explorer nodded. "I half expected this," he said in slow Temporal. "Do you understand me?"

The language had rusted in Tamberly. However— "I do. Welcome. You're what I've waited for these past . . . seven years, I think."

"I am Guillem Cisneros. Thirtieth century born, but with the Universarium of Halla." —in a milieu after time travel had been achieved and could therefore be done openly.

"And I, Stephen Tamberly, twentieth century, field historian for the Patrol."

Cisneros laughed. "A handshake is appropriate."

The villagers watched in dumbstruck awe.

"You were marooned here?" Cisneros asked redundantly.

"Yes. The Patrol must be told. Take me to a base."

"Certainly. I hid my vehicle about ten kilometers upstream." Cisneros hesitated. "My object was to pose as a wanderer, stay for a time, try to solve an archaeological mystery. I suspect you are the answer to it."

"I am," Tamberly said. "When I realized I was trapped unless help should come, I remembered the Valdivia ware."

The most ancient ceramics known in the western hemisphere, as of his home period. Almost a duplicate of the contemporaneous Jomon pottery in archaic Japan. The conventional explanation was that a fishing boat was blown across the Pacific, and the crew found refuge where they landed and taught the art to the natives. It didn't make much sense. More than eight thousand nautical miles to survive; and those men just happened to possess a set of intricate skills that in their society were the province of women. "So I provided it, and waited for somebody from the future to come looking."

He hadn't entirely violated the law for which the Patrol existed. It was necessarily flexible. Under the circumstances, his return was important.

"You were ingenious," Cisneros said. "How was your life here?"

"They're sweet people," Tamberly answered.

It will hurt, saying farewell to Aruna and the little ones. If I were a saint, I'd never have accepted her father's offer of her to me. Those seven years grew very long, and I didn't know if they would ever end. My family will miss me, but I'll leave them with such mana *that she'll soon get a new husband—a strong provider, probably Ula-mamo—and they'll live as well and gladly as any of their tribe. Which in its humble fashion is better than a lot of human beings live much farther up in time.*

He could not quite shed doubts and guilt, and knew he never would, but joy awakened. *I'm going home.*

25 MAY 1987

Soft light. Fine china, silverware, glass. I don't know if Ernie's is the top restaurant in San Franciso—matter of taste, that —but it's sure in the top ten. Except Manse has said he'd like to take me back to the 1970s before the owners of the Mingei-Ya retired.

He raises his sherry. "To the future," he says.

I do the same. "And the past." Clink. Magnificent stuff.

"We can talk now." When he smiles, his face kind of creases and isn't homely at all. "I'm sorry we couldn't earlier, aside from my calling to let you know your uncle's okay and invite you to dinner, but I've been hopping around like a flea on a griddle, tying up loose ends in this case."

Tease him "Couldn't you have done it and then ducked back several hours to let me off the hook?"

He goes serious. Oh, a lot of unspoken sorrow in his voice. "No. That would have cut things too close. We're allowed our pleasure jaunts in the Patrol, but not when they'd tangle events."

"Aw, Manse, I was kidding." Reach across the linen, pat his hand. "I'm getting a great meal out of this, am I not?" And a slinky dress on me, and my hair brushed just so.

"You've earned it," he says, more relieved than a big tough guy who's rambled from end to end of space-time reality ought to be.

Enough of this, for the time being. Too much to ask. "What about Uncle Steve? You told me how he released himself, but not where he is."

Manse chuckles. "That's hardly relevant, is it? A debriefing center somewhere and somewhen. He'll spend a long furlough with his wife in London before returning to duty. I'm sure he'll visit you and the rest of his kin. Be patient."

"And . . . afterward?"

"Well, we do have to terminate matters in a way that leaves the time-structure intact. We'll put Fray Esteban Tanaquil and Don Luis Castelar in that treasure house in Cajamarca, 1533, a minute or two after the Exaltationists bore them away. They'll exit on foot, and that will be that."

Frown. "Uh, you mentioned before that the guards got worried, looked inside, and found nobody. It caused a nasty sensation. Can you change that?"

He beams. "Smart lady! Excellent question. Yes, in such cases, when the past has been deformed, the Patrol does annul the events that flow from it. We restore the 'original' history, so to speak. As nearly as possible, anyhow."

Concern, oddly hurtful. "Luis, though. After what he's been through."

Manse takes a sip, twirls his glass between his fingers, stares into the amber it holds. "We considered inviting him to enroll, but his values are incompatible with ours. He will receive secrecy conditioning. It's harmless in itself, but makes a person unable to reveal anything about time travel. If he tries, and he will, his throat squeezes shut and his tongue locks on him. He'll soon stop trying."

Shake my head. "For him, terrible."

Manse stays calm. He's like a mountain, small shy flowers scattered around, but underneath them, that rock mass. "Would you rather we killed him, or wiped his memories and left him mindless? In spite of the woe he gave us, we bear no grudge."

"He does!"

"Uh-huh. He doesn't attack your uncle in the treasury, because Fray Tanaquil opens the door at once and tells the sentries that he's done. However, it wouldn't be wise keeping Fray Tanaquil around. In the morning he wanders off, as if to take a stroll while he meditates, and nobody sees him again. The soldiers miss him, he was such a nice fellow, and search, and fail, and decide at last that he came to grief in some unknown way. Don Luis tells them he knows nothing." Manse sighs. "We'll have to write off the holography project. Well, maybe someone can go to those objects when they were in their rightful places. We'll plant new agents to monitor the rest of Pizzaro's career. Your uncle will get a different assignment. He may well elect to go into administration, as his wife wishes he would."

I take a gently molten swallow from my glass. "What will—what became of Luis?"

He looks at me closely. "You do care about him, don't you?"

Heat in my cheeks. "Not in any, you know, romantic way. I wouldn't have him off the Christmas tree. But he's a person I've *known*."

He smiles afresh. "I see. Well, that's another thing I've been looking into this day. We keep tabs on Don Luis Castelar for the remainder of his life, just in case.

"He adapts fast. Continues as an officer of Pizarro's, distinguishes himself at Cuzco and in the fight against Almagro." With what inward-bitten grimness. "Finally, when the country is divvied up among the conquerors, he becomes a large land-owner. By the way, he's one of those few Spaniards who tried to get a reasonably square deal for the Indians. Later, when his wife has died, he takes holy orders and ends as a monk. He's had children by her, whose descendants flourish. Among them is a woman who marries a sea captain from North America. Yes, Wanda, the man you had that runa-round with is your ancestor."

Whew!

Recover after a minute. "Time travel indeed." All the ages open to wandering.

We ought to study our menus. But.

Be still, my heart, or whatever that foolish phrase is. I lean forward. Somehow I'm not afraid, not when he's looking at me like that. Only, my words stumble, while little cold lightnings run along my backbone. "Wh-wh-what about me, Manse? I know the secret too."

"Ah, yes," he says. How gently. "Typical of you, I think, that first you asked about the others. Well, you have your role to play out. We'll return you to your Galápagos island, dressed in the same clothes as then, a few minutes afterward. You'll rejoin your friends, finish your jaunt, fly from Baltra to that madhouse known as Guayaquil International Airport, and so home to California."

And then? Then?

"What happens next is for you to decide," he goes on. "You can take the conditioning. Not that we don't trust you, but the rule is firm. I repeat, it's painless and does no harm, and since I'm positive you'd never willingly betray us, it should make no noticeable difference. You can proceed with your twentieth-century life. Whenever you and your Uncle Steve get together privately, you'll be able to talk freely with him."

Stiffen the sinews, summon up the blood. "Have I got any other choice?

"Sure. You can become a time traveler yourself. You'd be a valuable recruit."

Unbelievable. Me? And yet I expected this. And yet. "I, I, I wonder how good a policewoman I'd make."

"Probably not very," I hear across the radiance. "You're too independent. But the Patrol's responsible for prehistoric as well as historic eras. That requires a knowledge of the environment, which requires field scientists. How'd you like to do your paleontology with living animals?"

Okay, okay, I disgrace myself. I jump to my feet and violate the peace of Ernie's with a war-whoop. Manse laughs.

Mammoths and cave bears and dodos, oh, my!